CW01024607

Loving
DANNY

Hilary Freeman is married to a musician and lives in Camden Town, North London. She is a regular contributor to *The Times*, the *Daily Mail* and the *Daily Express* and is an agony aunt for *CosmoGIRL!* She is also a relationship advisor for online advice service askTheSite and makes regular TV and radio appearances. This is her first novel.

HILARY FREEMAN

Piccadilly Press • London

To Steve, for believing

First published in Great Britain in 2006
by Piccadilly Press Ltd,
5 Castle Road, London NW1 8PR
www.piccadillypress.co.uk

Text copyright © Hilary Freeman, 2006

All rights reserved. No part of this publication may be reproduced, stored in a
retrieval system, or transmitted in any form or by any means, electronic,
mechanical, photocopying, recording or otherwise, without the prior
permission of the copyright owner.

The right of Hilary Freeman to be identified as Author of this work has been asserted
by her in accordance with the Copyright, Designs and Patents Act 1988

A catalogue record for this book is available from the British Library

ISBN-13: 978 1 85340 867 0

3 5 7 9 10 8 6 4 2

Printed and bound in Great Britain by Bookmarque Ltd
Typeset by M Rules, based on a design by Louise Millar
Cover design by Susan Hellard, Fielding Design and Simon Davis
Set in StempelGaramond and Carumba

The expression CosmoGIRL! is the registered trademark of the
National Magazine Company Ltd and the Hearst Corporation

Papers used by Piccadilly Press are produced from forests grown and
managed as a renewable resource, and which conform to the requirements of
recognised forestry accreditation schemes.

Chapter 1

The day I met Danny I had a hole in my tights. It appeared that morning, when I snagged them with the corner of a jagged fingernail as I pulled them up, and worked its way southwards as the day went on. By six p.m., when I made my way home from work, it had eaten its way past the hem of my skirt and stalled just above the cuff of my left, knee-high boot. No amount of skirt rearranging, leg crossing or bag repositioning could hide the hole from public view.

I mention this because it's one of the few things I remember about that day. I can't tell you what the weather was like or what I ate for breakfast. I have no idea what was on the news or what came in the post. Work is a blur. Before I met Danny, all I remember about that day is thinking how my mother would call me a trollop for wearing laddered tights to work, and cursing myself for still biting my nails, especially as I'd spent a fortune on expensive nail polish at Boots.

Isn't it weird how the truly significant days of your life often begin as the most banal? There you are, just minding your own business, doing something boring and ordinary like buying a Kit Kat or, in my case, catching the number 29 bus home from work and – boom! – the most momentous and life-changing event happens to you. You don't have time to rehearse or prepare or compose yourself. You don't even have time to change your tights.

My life-changing moment occurred shortly after ten past six, which was the last time I'd checked my watch. Danny (or the guy whose name I would later find out was Danny) got on the bus halfway up the high street. I was sitting at the back where there's more leg room, so I didn't notice him until he'd squeezed his way past the pushchairs and the strap-hangers and the men who territorially stretch their legs into the aisle, and made his way to the row of seats facing mine.

It was hardly the most romantic of beginnings. The very first words he said to me were, 'Uh, sorry,' as the bus choked and spluttered and sent him stumbling forwards on to my foot. I muttered something back and leaned down to brush his dusty footprint off my suede boot. When I looked up again he'd settled into his seat and was putting in some earphones.

I didn't want him to see me staring, so I turned to look out of the window. It was October and the nights were drawing in. Although it had been light when I left work, the sky was now the deep navy blue of dusk and the harsh lights on the bus were beginning to transform its windows into mirrors, reflecting everything inside. Soon, I could clearly see both my reflection and his.

He was fiddling with an iPod inside his jacket pocket. I tried to work out what type of music he'd be into. He was a wearing a beaten-up, vintage leather jacket, so old that the black looked almost brown, ripped jeans and a tour T-shirt for some obscure American band I'd only vaguely heard of. His hair was dark and almost shoulder-length and it looked as if he hadn't shaved for a day or two. He'd obviously tried hard to look like he wasn't trying too hard. But somehow, it worked.

I thought, *I bet he's listening to indie music.*

A few seconds later a familiar guitar riff began to bleed from his earphones. I smiled to myself; I was right.

It took me a moment to realise he was smiling too. He had very white, very even teeth and I liked the way his eyes crinkled up in the corners. Then, to my horror, I realised he was smiling at ME. I'd forgotten that when you look at somebody in a mirror they can see you too. It's like when you're a child and you close your eyes and really believe you've become invisible, but of course you haven't.

I watched my reflection turn crimson with embarrassment and I turned away from the window as quickly as I could, fumbling in my bag for something that wasn't there. I've never been any good at flirting. If someone makes eye contact with me I always feel so uncomfortable that I have to look away at once. If I try to smile I end up making an ugly grimace. It's even more discomforting if the person staring at me is cute. And he certainly was cute.

I also felt self-conscious about my clothes. Not the hole in my tights, which I was sure wouldn't bother him (it matched his tattered jeans, after all), but my boring wool coat, white shirt and navy, A-line skirt, which had actually belonged to my old school uniform.

I had started working at a solicitor's office just a week

after I'd finished my A-level exams and I still hadn't got round to shopping for new work clothes. To be honest, I hadn't really been bothered. I was saving all my money for university the following autumn, and, if I earned enough, a spot of travelling later in the year, before term started. Why waste money on drab suits to please my conservative boss, when I already had a wardrobe full of great clothes? I hadn't factored in wanting to impress a cool-looking guy on the way home.

There's only a limited period of time that you can pretend to be searching for something urgently, and remain convincing. Mine was running out fast. I was, however, aware that the moment I stopped peering in my bag my gaze would inevitably meet his. If I looked out of either window I'd see his mirror image; if I looked straight ahead, I'd be looking directly at the real him.

'Have you lost something?' he said.

Oh God.

'Um, yes, my ... er ... mobile,' I replied, my voice cracking with embarrassment and the knowledge of my lie. I'm almost as bad at lying as I am at flirting. My phone was, of course, beside me on my seat, tucked between my thigh and the armrest. I'd placed it there earlier for easy access.

I dared myself to look up at him, crossing my legs and smoothing my skirt down as I did so, in the hope that it would better conceal my phone. I felt certain everybody on the bus was looking at us; people don't talk to each other on public transport – it's one of those unwritten, universal rules that we must all be born knowing.

'Bummer,' he said. 'I'm always losing mine.'

His voice was deep and cigarette-croaky and he had a strange accent, which made him sound as if he was both well spoken and common at the same time.

'Yeah,' I said, playing along with my own story. 'I don't have half my numbers written down anywhere. My life is stored in that phone.'

He smiled again and shrugged his shoulders. I decided that he looked even more attractive in the flesh than in reflection. It might have been because of the slight bend of his nose. It's funny how different people can look when their features are reversed. I think it has something to do with how symmetrical you are. I'm always surprised when I see photos of myself and they don't look anything like the me I see in the mirror.

While we'd been talking I'd stopped looking at the road. Usually, I pressed the bell as soon as I saw the second-hand furniture shop at the end of my street. But on that fateful evening, by the time I noticed I was at my stop the bus doors were already open.

I leapt out of my seat, grabbing my bag and pushing past the other commuters who blocked the aisle, creating an obstacle course made up of bodies, umbrellas, briefcases and rucksacks. I reached the doors just as they slammed shut. Somebody pressed the bell urgently on my behalf and the doors flew open again, giving me just enough time to step on to the pavement before they closed emphatically behind me. Then, without pausing for breath, I turned into my street and broke into a half-walk, half-jog.

'Excuse me!'

The male voice came from behind me. I quickened my pace. It was now completely dark and the lighting on my street was notoriously poor – my dad had even written to the council about it. Whoever owned the voice could only be a beggar asking for change, or worse, a mugger or a rapist.

'Excuse me! *Hello!*'

Something about the voice sounded familiar.

'SLOW DOWN!' he shouted. 'I'VE GOT YOUR PHONE!'

Still walking, I swung round, at the same time feeling for my phone inside my bag. It wasn't there. In my hurry, I hadn't picked it up off the seat. Panic turned to relief then to embarrassment as I was struck by a second realisation: the voice belonged to HIM.

If I'd been a cartoon character, like the ones I grew up watching every Saturday morning when my parents were still in bed, I would have screeched to a halt, leaving track-lines in the pavement behind me. Instead, I clumsily stumbled, tripping over my feet as I came to an unplanned stop.

'God, you don't half walk fast,' he said, finally catching up with me. 'Who did you think I was, some mad axe-man?'

'No, of course not,' I said, with little conviction. The truth was, he was a stranger on a bus. We'd had a thirty-second conversation. He *could* have been a mad axe murderer for all I knew, albeit a very cute one.

He handed me my phone. 'It must have been on your seat all along,' he said, smiling so broadly and cheekily that

I knew he had caught me out. I felt myself reddening. 'I saw it when you rushed off. Lucky, that.'

There was a pause. It was, in retrospect, a very important pause, the ideal chance for him to say goodbye and walk away and never see me again. If he had taken advantage of the opportunity that pause afforded him, he'd have been forever just 'the guy on the bus who kindly gave me back my lost phone' – a bit-part player instead of the lead actor.

But he didn't. Still sporting that mischievous, dazzling grin, he said, 'My name's Danny, by the way. And you are?'

'I'm, er, Naomi.' Until I actually said it, I hadn't been sure if I'd give him my real name or a made-up one.

'So where are you off to in such a hurry, Naomi?'

I really liked the way he pronounced my name, emphasising the 'o' and not the 'a', like most people do. When your name has as many vowel sounds as mine, there's a big margin for error.

'I'm just going home,' I said, remembering again that he was a stranger. I didn't want him to know where I lived. I rearranged my bag on my shoulder, to indicate that I was about to start walking again.

He understood. 'Sure,' he said. He reached into his jacket pocket and pulled something out. It was a piece of paper. 'I'm playing a gig at The Bunker, next Thursday – why don't you come along? Bring a friend, if you like. I'll put your name down on the door.'

He pressed the paper into my hand. His fingers were long and the tips rough – a guitarist's fingers.

'See you, Naomi,' he said, with the self-assurance of

someone who knew that he would. 'I'd better get going –
you made me get off the bus about four stops early.'

He smiled, playfully, then turned and walked away. I
opened my mouth to shout 'goodbye' or 'thank you' after him,
but he was too quick for me. Soon he had vanished into the
darkness.

I unfolded the piece of paper. It was a flyer.

New Band Night at The Bunker
Thursday, October 28th @ 7p.m.
Live on Stage:
The Ring Pulls
Collateral Damage
Billy Franklin and the Hot Press
The Wonderfulls
Dandelion
Tickets £5 in advance – available from
www.bunkermusic.co.uk
or £7 on the door

He hasn't told me the name of his band, I thought, unzipping
my bag and placing the flyer inside.

It would probably have remained there for weeks,
nestling amongst the receipts, crumbs and grubby, loose
mints, if it hadn't been for one thing: from that moment on,
I couldn't stop thinking about Danny.

Chapter 2

When I reached the house I noticed that Mum's car was parked in the drive. I didn't feel like recounting my boring day at work – just living it was tedious enough – so I let myself in as quietly as I could, hung up my coat, unzipped my boots and crept straight upstairs to my bedroom.

I had slept in that room since I was six months old, but it didn't feel like mine any more. It belonged to someone younger, someone who liked pink, fluffy cushions and curled-up posters of faded pop stars whose names I had all but forgotten. That naïve and unsophisticated girl enjoyed skipping and Scrabble and playing with dolls. She had become an embarrassment; I didn't want to share my space with her. Now I wanted a room with freshly painted white walls, neat blinds and a sofa. But there was no point redecorating – my bedroom had no place in my plans for the future. Why waste my energy? I'd be leaving home for university in under a year.

I peeled off my tights (or what was left of them) and dropped them into the bin under my desk, watching as the lid swung back and forth in rhythmic applause. I couldn't wait to get out of my work clothes and into my jeans. Only four months into my placement and I was already beginning to wonder whether I really wanted a future career in law. Still, Dad had used his contacts to get me a gap-year job with a reputable firm and I knew I should be grateful. 'It's a great opportunity,' he had said, in his most headmaster-like voice. 'You'll be streets ahead of the other students and it will help you get a job after university.' But I didn't feel grateful. I felt trapped, as though my life's path had been laid out in front of me and I would have to walk along it, without any say in its direction.

'Naomi? Is that you?' Mum was coming up the stairs, the sensible heels of her court shoes clip-clopping on the wooden slats.

'I'm just getting changed,' I shouted back, willing her not to come in. I could sense her loitering outside the door, her hand poised above the door handle.

'All right, then.' She sounded disappointed. 'But make sure you come down for dinner. Dad will be home soon.'

'Sure.'

I couldn't hide my lack of enthusiasm. Over the past few years family dinners had become an ordeal – and it had nothing to do with Mum's cooking. My parents didn't believe in eating in front of the TV. We had to sit around the table all together, making polite small talk about our school or work days and offering 'intelligent' comments on the day's news. I think Mum and Dad saw it as some sort of family-bonding exercise, a way of ensuring my younger sister Emily, who was sixteen, and I confided in them. Of course, we never, ever told them anything interesting or important about our lives.

And that night, I had absolutely no intention of telling Mum and Dad that I'd met a guy named Danny on the number 29.

But I did want to tell someone. I was already beginning to forget what Danny looked like and what he'd said. Talking about him would make him real again. I felt for his flyer in my bag and unfolded it, brushing off the crumbs. It was just a meaningless list of band names. Reading it three times didn't help either.

'What's that?'

I jumped. Emily had come into my room. She never knocked. Usually, I'd have been irritated, but this time I was glad of the opportunity to talk.

'It's a flyer. For a gig.'

'Cool. Who's playing?'

I handed her the piece of paper and she studied it for a second, chewing her lip and then frowning dismissively.

'Never heard of any of them. Where did you get it?'

'A guy gave it to me. He's in one of the bands. I met him on the bus.'

Now she was interested. She sat down on my bed, crossing her legs. 'Really? What was he like?'

'He was cute.' I felt myself reddening. 'I didn't speak to him for long. Er, he was nice,' I said and smiled, unintentionally. 'He had something about him. I'm not sure if he'd have been your type. Scruffy – you know, an indie boy. He was looking at me and I was embarrassed. So I sort of lost my phone – even though I really did know where it was – and he found it and gave it back to me.'

'God Naomi, anyone would think you'd never met a guy before. You gonna go to the gig, then?'

I shrugged, trying to regain my composure. Why do I always ramble like that when I'm nervous? 'Maybe.'

'You've got to go. You never go out any more.'

It was true. Since my best mate Debbie had gone to university in Manchester and Natasha, Holly and my other friends had gone travelling, my social life had all but disappeared. Even my parents were beginning to take pity on me, offering me tickets to theatre performances and saying I could join them for bridge games (which, I must point out, I declined, and not always politely). Taking a gap year had seemed like such a good idea when all I'd thought about was the money I'd earn and the work experience I'd gain. I hadn't anticipated the loneliness, the sense that I was the one missing out. How could I have let my parents persuade me to turn down a round-the-world airline ticket for a bus pass and a day job? Still, I didn't want my suddenly sophisticated little sister, with her diary full of parties and youth clubs and sleepovers, reminding me of how boring I'd become.

'OK, I'll go. Do you want to come?'

'I suppose,' she said, trying not to sound too keen. She flicked her perfectly straight, blond hair. Why hadn't she inherited the 'frizz gene' like me? 'Yeah, all right. If I'm not busy.'

I didn't like her superior tone. 'It's on a school night, Emily,' I said, bitchily. I wanted to make it clear that I was still her big sister, still more worldly and mature. 'You'll have to ask Mum and Dad for permission. What was it you came in for, anyway?'

She looked hurt. Awkwardly, she climbed off my bed, unsure where to put herself. Now she was sheepish. 'Doesn't matter.'

'No, really. Did you want something?' I tried to make my voice as warm as possible. I hadn't meant to sound so mean. I really wanted to go to Danny's gig and I knew I couldn't – or wouldn't – go alone. I needed her to come with me. It might even be fun. Emily may have been a poor replacement for Debbie or Natasha or any of my other friends, but the fact was my friends weren't around. Given my circumstances, she was my only choice. And she knew it.

'You know that black halter-neck top you've got, the vintage one?'

I stiffened, certain of what was coming next.

'Can I borrow it for Andy's party on Saturday? I reckon it will look cool with my new trousers.'

She was, if you'll pardon the pun, trying it on. That top was my favourite – the most unique and flattering item in my wardrobe. I'd found it at an antiques market a year earlier and had bargained the stallholder down until I could just about afford it (it had cleaned out my Saturday job savings). It was made from the softest silk, with jet beading on the halter part and, because of the way it was cut – I think they call it 'on the bias' – it made my waist look tiny.

Emily could have asked to borrow any other piece of clothing and I would have been more than happy to oblige. But not that top. And not for a sixteenth birthday party. It would inevitably come back covered in beer (and maybe vomit) and reeking of cigarette smoke. What's more, the top wouldn't even suit Emily. It was designed to be worn by a woman with boobs and curves like me, not one as angular and flat chested as my sister.

'Of course you can borrow it,' I said, smiling through gritted teeth. If it meant that much to her, I could give in, just this once. 'But please be careful with it. And get it cleaned afterwards.'

'Thanks, Nay!' Emily beamed at me, enjoying her little victory. She was well aware that I don't like being called 'Nay', but all her friends shortened each other's names and now doing the same to mine had become an unbreakable habit. She walked back over to the bed and made herself comfortable again. 'So, what are you going to wear to this gig, then?'

'God knows. I haven't given it any thought. Maybe my black halter neck, if,' I hammered home my point, 'if it's still in one piece!'

'Let's face it, Nay. If he liked you in your work gear he's gonna be pleasantly surprised whatever you wear next time.'

'Perhaps I'll borrow something of yours,' I teased. I never borrowed Emily's clothes. Aside from the fact that most of them were too tight, I didn't much like her style. She dressed to show off her midriff and her legs – neither of which were my best features – and she wore lots of slogan T-shirts in bright colours, which I thought looked cheap.

'If you want,' she said, without irony.

Downstairs, the front door slammed shut. Dad was

home. I knew that in exactly two minutes Mum would be calling us down for dinner. I could have set my watch by it. Emily pushed herself up. 'Suppose we'd better go down,' she said, sighing. 'Get it over with.'

I rolled my eyes at her. 'OK, but don't mention anything about the gig. I'm not in the mood for an interrogation tonight.'

We went downstairs together. Dad was already sitting at the kitchen table. He'd taken off his glasses and was rubbing his eyes with the side of his hand. His bald scalp gleamed under the fluorescent strip lighting.

'Hello, girls,' he said, without looking up. 'Did you have a productive day?'

His question wasn't addressed to anyone in particular, so we both muttered affirmatively.

'I'm just going to help Mum,' I said, sensing an opportunity for escape. Emily screwed up her face at me. She hadn't been quick enough, this time.

Mum was juggling steaming pots and pans at the other end of our L-shaped kitchen. 'Ah, Naomi,' she said, gratefully. 'Would you help me serve the food and take it in?'

She had cooked spaghetti, with bolognese sauce for herself and Dad, and a vegetable sauce for me and Emily. I'd been vegetarian since I was eleven; Emily was just a fussy eater and didn't like mince.

Dinner passed without incident. Between mouthfuls, Dad told us what he thought was a funny anecdote about a man in the accounts department at work who'd left his travelcard on the train and had been fined, or something like that. I'm afraid I wasn't listening properly, so I can't repeat the story. Mum told Emily off for getting a C in her maths test and informed her she wouldn't be allowed out the night before a test again. She also told us she'd got a new piano pupil, whom she'd be teaching on Tuesday evenings at six. Dad asked after Mr Stevens, my boss and his occasional golf partner. I said I hadn't spoken to him that day, as I'd been left in the photocopying room on my own with a waist-high pile of folders to work my way through. I moaned that I could still see the flash of the machine every time I closed my eyes and now probably had radiation poisoning. Dad tutted, 'Well, we all have to start somewhere.'

My mind kept drifting to Danny. I wondered if he was eating dinner somewhere too, and with whom. He seemed too self-assured to live with his parents. Did he live on his own or did he share a flat with mates? I pictured him sitting in a bedsit, surrounded by guitars and CDs. I wished I hadn't been so keen to rush off. Perhaps he would have asked me if I fancied a coffee, there and then. We would have gone to the greasy spoon on the corner of Murray Street and talked till it closed. Then—

'Naomi, I said did you want some fruit? Naomi!' Mum looked exasperated. I shook my head.

'Don't worry about Naomi, Mum,' Emily said, smiling cryptically. 'She's got a lot on her mind. Isn't that right, Nay?'

'Shut up, Em,' I muttered, under my breath. I felt foolish. Danny probably hadn't given me another thought. I was merely a potential audience member for his gig, a clumsy girl who couldn't even manage to get off a bus without forgetting her phone. He almost certainly had a girlfriend, or a string of beautiful girlfriends. I was angry with myself for reading so much into nothing. How had my life become so mundane, so empty, that a momentary encounter with an attractive guy could make me fantasise about a future together?

I excused myself from the table and went back upstairs, leaving Emily to help with the washing-up. There were at least three hours to fill before bedtime. It was strange how long the evenings seemed now; last year, with homework to complete and friends to see, I'd felt I never had enough time. It was as if I'd been running on a treadmill that had suddenly stopped, sending me flying aimlessly. Maybe, it now occurred to me, I hadn't been as in control of my life as I'd believed. All my agendas, all my goals, had been set by school or by my friends. My social life had been handed to me on a plate. I had never had to be proactive. But if I was going to get through the next year I'd have to take risks, find things I enjoyed, and force myself to go out and be more independent. The only problem was I didn't know where to start.

There was nothing on TV, so I decided to listen to some music. I put on my favourite CD, a compilation that an ex-boyfriend, Mark, had made for me in the summer after our GCSEs. It was an eclectic mixture of songs that he'd downloaded or copied from his own collection: contemporary guitar bands plus some 1960s folk, 80s pop and 90s dance music. Unfortunately for Mark, I'd enjoyed listening to his CD far more than spending time with him.

For about an hour, I lay on my bed with my eyes closed. Downstairs, my family were going about their routines. Emily had popped out to a friend's house. Dad was in his study, doing paperwork. Mum was giving a piano lesson to a neighbour's very unmusical child. The cacophonous notes kept bleeding through the ceiling, jarring with the melodies on my CD. Mum must have been seething with frustration; she was such a perfectionist, especially when it came to music. At least she was busy. It seemed that everyone else had something to do, a purpose. Everyone except me.

Shut up, Naomi. I had to stop feeling sorry for myself – it wasn't an appealing trait and I knew it wouldn't get me anywhere. I sat up and gazed at the photo on my bedside table. It showed me, Debbie, Natasha and Holly, all grinning broadly, our arms wrapped around each other. Funny to think it had only been taken a few months before. We were inseparable. Now, Debbie was in Manchester, Natasha in New York, and as for Holly, who knew? Her last e-mail, which I'd received a month before, had come from Sydney. In it she said she had met a guy and was planning to travel to Indonesia with him.

Debbie hadn't called me for a few days. When she'd left for Manchester we agreed that we'd take it in turns to phone each other on alternate nights, but it hadn't worked out that way. We were on such different schedules, she might as well have been on the other side of the world too. I was up at seven a.m., she rarely went to bed before three or four. I had to be asleep by eleven, not long after she'd gone out for the night. She got up during my lunch hour.

Although strictly it was Debbie's turn to ring, I wanted

to talk to her that minute. It was nine o'clock; she might still be in her room. I took my mobile out of my bag and dialled. I didn't even have to look what I was doing – she was number one on speed-dial.

Her phone rang at least ten times before she picked up. 'Naomi, hi!' There was so much background noise, I could hardly hear her. 'I'm in the Union bar. Hold on a sec.' I heard her apologising to someone, then the background noise subsided and she came back on the line.

'Sorry, just had to go outside. What are you up to?' she asked.

'Oh, you know, this and that.' I tried to hide how world-weary I felt. 'What about you?'

She sounded excited. 'I'm just having a few drinks in the Union, then me and some of my mates from Hall are going clubbing in town. There's this great place that basically has a happy hour till midnight. And girls get in half price. Maybe we can go when you come up to stay. Hold on a second . . .'

I heard her saying hello to someone and then she must have hugged them because their voices suddenly sounded muffled. 'Sorry about that. Just this guy from my tutorial group. I think he's had a few too many. So, what have you been doing again?'

I knew I had nothing to tell her except that I'd met Danny. But she was meeting new guys every day; my brief encounter wouldn't impress her.

'I sort of met a guy today,' I volunteered, after a long pause. 'He's called Danny.'

'Oh, Naomi! That's great!' she cried. 'Are you going to see him again?' I'd left out the part about the bus and she'd concluded we'd already been on a date.

'Yes,' I half lied. 'We're going out next Thursday. Well, I'm going to see his band play.'

'That's great, Naomi,' she said again. I could tell she was only half-concentrating. 'Listen, I've got to go now. But I promise I'll call you tomorrow. You can tell me all about him then.'

I'd hardly managed to say goodbye before she hung up. I felt a little annoyed that she hadn't had time for me. But, if I was honest with myself, I knew that I'd be the same if I were in her position. Why on earth, I asked myself again, had I chosen to take a gap year? Why hadn't I realised I'd be left behind? The truth was I was jealous that Debbie was having such a good time, and scared that she'd replace me with a new best friend. I felt this more acutely every time we spoke, every time she mentioned someone she'd met in the coffee bar or in the queue for a lecture. I was so self-conscious about my lack of interesting news I was sure she'd soon discover what a boring person I really was.

Even if I'd known where to go to meet new people, I've never been the sort of person who can walk into a room, march up to a stranger and introduce myself. I don't know what to talk about, or how much eye contact to make and I'm not very good at judging when to move on to someone else. Always too polite, I usually end up getting stuck all night with the creepy, sweaty-palmed guy who nobody else wants to talk to. I had hoped that I might make some new friends at work, but although everyone was friendly enough, they were all much older than me and many of them were married with children. They treated me like the 'work experience girl', which, of course, I was.

I've got other friends, I told myself. OK, maybe they weren't such close friends, but I could still call them, couldn't I? What about Dee? She had been in my class at school and, like me, had stayed in London. But unlike me, it wasn't out of choice: poor Dee had got such bad marks in her A-levels that she was having to retake. Knowing there was someone worse off than me made me feel a little better. I believe my old German teacher would have called that feeling *Schadenfreude*.

I didn't have Dee's number on speed-dial, so I had to look in my phone's address book for it. Nonchalantly, I started scrolling through the Ds: Dad, mobile; Dad, work; Danny; Debbie . . .

Danny? I didn't know anyone called Danny. Did I? My heart began to pound. The cartoon 'me' did an exaggerated double-take, reacting with bug-eyed, wide-jawed surprise.

No, it couldn't be . . . could it?

There was only one possible explanation. Somehow, in the short time between chasing me from the bus and giving me back my phone, Danny had typed his name and number into my address book. He could only have done it because he wanted me to know he liked me. Maybe he even wanted me to call him. For an instant, I thought about doing it and then, just as quickly, decided against it. I told myself it was because I didn't want to appear too keen, but I knew, really, that it was fear that stopped me: fear of a stilted, silence-laden conversation; fear of spoiling the delicious anticipation of what might be.

I never did get around to calling Dee.

And I didn't sleep a wink that night.

Chapter 3

From the outside, The Bunker looks just like any other old pub on any high street in Britain. Its brickwork is decorated with overlapping graffiti, which nobody will ever be able to wash off entirely, and the bright green paintwork on the windows and doors is now chipped and peeling, exposing the wood beneath. A long time ago, someone – a landlord hoping for a different sort of clientele, perhaps – hung flower baskets along its frontage. But that landlord has clearly long since gone and the flowers have withered and died, leaving a mess of weeds and straw, which partially obscure the pub sign.

Strictly speaking, the pub is named The King's Arms, but it has become known for the music venue in its bowels and now everybody calls it 'The Bunker'. You don't even have to go into the main part of the pub to get to the venue (only old men drink in the pub); The Bunker has its own door at the side. Then it's down a long flight of stairs, which reek of stale beer and urine, to a dimly lit basement where you'll find another bar and a cavernous room with a stage at the far end.

I'd been to The Bunker many times before, but I'd never noticed just how dilapidated it was until the night of Danny's gig. That's probably because I'd never spent so much time standing outside it. Emily and I arrived unfashionably early, at seven p.m. It was Danny's fault (and mine too, for not having the guts to call or even text and ask); he hadn't told me which band he was in, so I had to be there for the start. The doors had not yet opened, so we loitered in the street outside, shuffling from foot to foot and repeatedly checking our watches and our mobile phones to make it look as though we were waiting for someone. I was on high alert with nerves, jumping every time a car drew up or a group of people walked past. If anybody even half resembling Danny approached in the distance, my stomach lurched.

I hadn't got much work done that day. I'd daydreamed my way through the filing and the photocopying, barely saying a word to anyone. I had left the office the moment I could, running for the bus and cursing every time it stopped at the traffic lights or stayed too long at a stop. I knew I only had half an hour to get changed, do my make-up and rush out again.

Fortunately, I had laid out my chosen outfit on my bed that morning. It had taken me the whole of the previous evening to decide what to wear. I'd modelled every garment in my wardrobe for Emily, calling her in and out of my room until she was so frustrated that she would have endorsed an orange shellsuit. It seemed as if everything I possessed was either too tight, too baggy, too warm or too revealing for the gig. My halter neck looked too dressy, jeans and a T-shirt too casual. We'd settled on black jeans and a green camisole top, with a black cotton cardigan to hide my chubby arms. Of course, it still didn't feel right, but it would have to do.

Hanging round outside the bunker, Emily was bored.

She pulled out a packet of cigarettes from her bag and lit one up. She expected me to looked shocked and say, 'I didn't know you smoked!' I think that's half the reason she did it – to provoke a reaction. Instead, I called her bluff and asked if I could have one too.

'I thought you had given up, Nay,' she said, annoyed that she had failed in her attempt to impress.

'Yes, I have, sort of. But I need something to do to try and calm my nerves,' I replied. 'And it's bloody freezing out here. I smiled, patting her arm. 'Don't worry, I'll buy you some more later.'

She beamed. I wasn't going to tell on her. We were becoming allies, friends even.

In the end, it had been surprisingly easy to persuade my parents to allow Emily to come with me. I'd cornered Mum when Dad wasn't around, knowing that she'd approve of any outing involving music. The conversation had gone something like this:

Me, in my sweetest tone: 'Mum, I really fancy hearing some music and a band I like is playing on Thursday night.'

Mum, falling for it: 'That's a lovely idea, Naomi. What's the band called?'

Me, worried that she might invite herself along: 'You wouldn't have heard of them. They're new.'

Mum, disappointed: 'Oh. Are you going with some friends from work?'

Me, looking mournful: 'No, it's not really their scene. Could Emily come with me? I'll make sure she does her homework first and we won't be late.'

Mum, looking pleased: 'It's nice that the two of you want to spend some time together. I'm sure it'll be OK with your dad.'

See? Easy. Emily hadn't done her homework, but we'd worry about that another day.

Three cigarettes later, at quarter to eight, somebody finally unlocked the doors to The Bunker. We loitered a little longer, so as not to appear too eager, then made our way down the stairs. A guy with greasy blond hair was manning the front desk, a makeshift table which blocked the way to the bar. Obviously worried about the night's takings, he looked happy to see us.

'We're on the guest list,' said Emily brightly.

'Name?' asked the blond guy.

'Naomi,' I said, pushing myself in front of Emily. I wasn't sure if she was too young to be there and I didn't want her drawing attention to herself. 'Plus one. Danny said he'd put us down.'

'Danny Evans?'

I had no more idea what Danny's surname was than what band he was in. 'Um, yes,' I muttered, hoping I'd got the right Danny.

The blond guy picked up a biro and scrolled his way down the typed list in front of him. Then he scrolled back up again. For a moment I feared humiliation. Had Danny forgotten about me? Was I supposed to have rung him to say I was coming?

'Ah, yes. You must be "the lovely Naomi",' he said,

smirking, as he turned the sheet of paper around so that I could see it too. There, in black type, were the words *the lovely Naomi*. A burning wave of crimson spread upwards from my neck, to my cheeks and to my ears.

'How cheesy,' tutted Emily, under her breath. *Or cheeky*, I thought to myself, secretly delighted that Danny thought me 'lovely' and didn't care who knew it. *There's a fine line.*

'Um, thanks,' I spluttered to the guy on the desk, glad it was so dark in there. I tried to push my way past the table.

'Hang on, I need to stamp you!' The blond guy smiled again, this time more kindly. He grabbed my hand, clumsily, and impressed it with an inked rubber stamp. Now the word *Bunker* was indelibly printed across my knuckles. I knew it would take at least three days of scrubbing to wash it off.

'The Wonderfulls won't be on till about ten,' he said. 'Go and get yourselves a drink.'

The bar was empty, so for once I didn't have to jump up and down to attract attention. Barmen never notice me; I grow bored of waiting to be served, lose eye contact and end up people-watching instead. I bought myself a glass of white wine and a Diet Coke for Emily. When I gave it to her she looked dismissive, but she didn't say anything. We could both tell that the barman had seen beneath the layers of make-up that she'd so expertly applied and clocked that she was underage.

As we sipped our drinks the bar slowly filled up. There were lots of overweight, balding, middle-aged men with ponytails and tattoos, several skinheads and a big group of indie kids with hennaed hair and second-hand leather jackets – the sort of odd mix of people that could only ever come together in one place on a 'new band' night.

'I haven't seen this many ponytails since the *Horse of the Year show*,' I joked.

To amuse ourselves, we played 'spot the fan', using my crumpled flyer to try to match the people in the bar to the band names. We decided that the ponytails followed Billy Franklin and the Hot Press, the skinheads were there for Collateral Damage, and the indie kids either The Wonderfulls or Dandelion. As for the poor Ring Pulls, we concluded that their fans must have deserted them.

By the time the first band came on and we were ushered next door to the room with the stage, I felt much more relaxed. It had a little to do with the wine, of course, but it was nice to be out, and Emily was actually quite good company. Every time I started fretting about Danny, she'd wink and refer to me as 'the lovely Naomi', making me crack up. She was also better than me at dissuading guys from joining us at our table. She'd just give them a withering look and they'd be off.

Once the music started, however, the evening went downhill. The Ring Pulls were dreadful – their entire set sounded as if each member of the band was playing a different song, simultaneously. When Collateral Damage came on – a thrash metal outfit whose shaved heads matched their fans' – we had to flee for the safety of the bar, or risk losing our hearing for ever. We didn't even bother to go back in for Billy Franklin and the Hot Press.

'Maybe this was a bad idea,' I said. I was beginning to feel anxious again. I also half feared that The Wonderfulls might be as bad as the other groups. 'I'm ready to go, if you are.'

'You are joking, aren't you?' said Emily. 'You've chewed my ear off about Danny for the past week, made me stand outside like an idiot, sit through two hours of hell, and now, a few minutes before he comes on stage, you want to leave. No way. Even if you don't want to stay to see Danny, I most certainly do.'

'Wow, that told me,' I conceded. 'OK, we'll stay. But don't blame me if The Wonderfulls are, er, terrible.'

Part of me – the cowardly part – actually wanted Danny's band to be an embarrassment. That way, Emily and I could leave halfway through his set and I wouldn't have to face him afterwards. I could delete his name from my phone, tear up his flyer and forget I'd ever bumped into him. Life would continue as normal. Normal and uncomplicated.

In truth, I feared Danny would be disappointed. I was afraid that the reality of me would not live up to his memory of me, just as I feared that the image of Danny, which I had stored in my mind since our meeting, had been enhanced by hope and expectation. I suppose it's not really possible to be nostalgic about something that has not yet happened. But that's the closest I can get to describing how I felt.

There was a sudden exodus of indie kids from the bar. 'Come on, then,' Emily said, dragging me up from my seat. 'It's show time!'

'Don't make me stand near the front, please, Em,' I

begged. I needn't have worried – we couldn't get near the stage. *I* might never have heard of The Wonderfulls before, but they appeared to have collected a large and loyal following. I felt a stab of jealousy when I realised that most of the fans were girls.

The lights dimmed and four male silhouettes appeared on the stage. The crowd whooped. There was a drummer, a keyboard player, a bass guitarist and a lead guitarist. For a second, I was confused: neither of the guitarists resembled Danny. Had he cut his hair? Was he shorter than I remembered? Then, as a spotlight hit the stage, a lone figure walked out to the front, a guitar slung over his shoulder, and took his place at the microphone. The crowd whooped again, louder this time. There could be no mistake: Danny was standing before me.

Emily nudged me. 'Is that him?' she mouthed above the cheering. 'He's gorgeous.'

My stomach was in knots, but I couldn't help grinning. 'Yes, that's him.'

Emily poked me in the ribs, as if to signal her approval and, perhaps, her surprise that someone so good-looking and charismatic might be interested in her older sister. I could barely believe it myself.

I had been carrying a single, blurry picture of Danny around in my mind ever since we'd met on the bus – a snapshot of a cute but slightly scruffy guy. Looking up at him on the stage gave me a whole new perspective. His legs were longer than I recalled, and his jaw squarer. Perhaps it was the well-cut, striped suit jacket that he was wearing over his

T-shirt, but his shoulders looked broader too. Standing in front of me was a rock star, as unobtainable as the ones in the pictures in my old magazines. Although I fancied Danny even more than I had expected to, he had become a total stranger again and it unnerved me.

Watching Danny perform, it was clear that he was in his element. He commanded the stage, moving from one side to the other with an effortless grace. It was his territory; the bands that had played earlier were merely his warm-up. Each time the crowd roared his eyes lit up. He knew he had every one of us – men and women alike – eating out of the palm of his hand. And the knowledge empowered him. He was no longer six feet tall – he was a giant, as high and wide as the room itself. I'd never really understood what stage presence meant until I watched Danny that night.

His voice, too, was a revelation. Nothing like the low drawl of his speaking voice, it was strong and raw and rich, with a haunting lilt. He sang effortlessly, soaring between the high and low notes, never running out of breath even when he flung his body about the stage. His voice was an untrained tenor, a rock voice – the type my mother would have loved to mould and shape – but, to my ears, all the better for its crudeness. I couldn't make out all the lyrics, but the songs were dark – full of allusions to love, death and loss. Most began gently, with a melodic keyboard or guitar riff, building up into a fantastic frenzy of thrashing guitars and crashing drums.

And all the while, I felt as if Danny was singing only to me. I knew it wasn't rational – the lights were out and I was in the middle of a packed crowd, squashed up to Emily on one side, my face pressed into a stranger's back – but wherever he stood on the stage he seemed to be looking directly into my eyes. No one else existed.

The Wonderfulls' set lasted forty-five minutes. Usually when I see a band I don't know, I start fidgeting and checking my watch, hoping every song is the last. When you don't recognise any of the songs, they all tend to blend into one. But I was so mesmerised by Danny that when he said, 'This is our final song,' and his loyal fans cheered at the opening chords, I actually felt a tinge of disappointment.

When the last cheers had died down and The Wonderfulls had disappeared backstage, the lights came on and Emily said, 'We'd better get to the bar, then, and talk to Danny.' For a few seconds I stood rooted to the spot, unable – and unwilling – to break out of my trance. She nudged me. 'Come on, that's what we're here for.' I let her lead me through the remnants of the crowd. She was excited and star-struck, keen to meet Danny and pleased to have a reason to do so.

'Can we go to the loos first, please, Em?' I asked, my voice hoarse from shouting over the din. I felt sick with nerves, vulnerable and unattractive. I was sure that my make-up had run and that my hair was lank and frizzy.

Emily sighed. She could read my mind. 'OK, but you look great, honestly,' she said.

As always, there was a queue outside the Ladies'. By the time we came out – freshly powdered, our lip-gloss reapplied – the bar was starting to clear out for the final act.

The coward in me prayed that Danny had already left, but I saw him at once, standing in the far corner with a bottle of beer in his hand. He was surrounded by a group of girls, each one prettier than the last. One of them was standing tight up against him and he was smiling at her, nodding his head and occasionally laughing. Another girl, dark and petite, rushed up to him and kissed him on both cheeks. Someone else tugged playfully at his T-shirt.

I hung back, waiting for my moment, ignoring Emily's nudges.

'You're going to miss your chance. What are you playing at?' she moaned. I was irritated, as much with myself as with Emily. I knew I didn't have the courage to walk up to Danny and say hello, and I felt stupid standing there without a drink, exposed. But my feet were glued to the floor, my mouth so dry that my lips were sticking to my teeth.

'I'm sorry Emily, but I just can't do this,' I said finally. The rest of The Wonderfulls had joined Danny's party and he was now engrossed in conversation with the bass player.

Emily looked defeated. 'Don't blame me when you wake up tomorrow and you realise you've blown your chance with him,' she said, refusing to look me in the eye. She turned and made for the exit, not caring if I was behind her. I paused for a moment, and then began to follow.

'Naomi!'

I stopped dead. It was Danny's unmistakable voice.

'Naomi, wait!' he shouted. Before I could turn round his hand was on my shoulder. 'You're always rushing off, aren't you?' he said, smiling. His face glistened with sweat from his performance and his eyes were bright with exhilaration. 'Am I going to have to chase after you all the time? You do know, it's really not my style.'

'I'm sorry,' I stuttered, unsure what to say or do. I was paralysed, my body still headed for the door, my neck twisted round so my face could meet his. Emily had disappeared up the stairs and would be waiting for me outside, annoyed and impatient.

Danny's eyes bore into mine with an intensity that thrilled me, but at the same time made me uncomfortable. I felt vulnerable, as if I was naked, and I had to look away, momentarily. When I looked back Danny's gaze was unbroken.

'I'm so glad you came,' he said, gently removing his hand. 'Did you enjoy it?'

'Oh, yes,' I said, awkwardly moving my body so that I was standing straight in front of him. He was unbearably close and my heart was beating rapidly, my face glowing red. 'You were great, really great.' I instantly regretted using the word 'great'. Like 'nice', it was just a meaningless platitude. But my entire vocabulary seemed to have vanished into a chasm in my brain.

He didn't appear to notice. 'Why didn't you come and find me? I saw you standing there with your friend. I thought you'd come over.'

'She's my sister,' I said, embarrassed. 'You had so many people around you . . . your band . . . all those girls.'

He looked as if he was about to laugh. 'Ah. But none of those girls has my number in their phone.'

I felt an involuntary smile spreading across my face at

the memory of what he'd done. 'Really? Oh.'

'It was hardly subtle now, was it, Naomi?'

'No.' I laughed. 'You're lucky I had to call someone beginning with 'D', or I might never have found it.'

There was an uncomfortable silence, as we both fumbled for something to say next. I was aware that Danny's drummer had come up behind me and was motioning to his watch. Danny brushed him off; he wouldn't take his eyes off me. 'Hang on a second, Pete,' he said. He smiled at me again. 'Listen, I've got to help the guys pack up our stuff. What are you doing tomorrow night?'

Nothing, I thought, with absolute certainty. A few months ago it would have been a very different story. Back then, my schedule was so full with parties and shopping trips and study that I had been forced to become an expert at juggling times and people.

'I think I'm free,' I said, looking up to the ceiling as though I was picturing a full diary and wondering if I could fit him into it. I didn't want him to know about my non-existent social life. 'Yes, I'm free,' I repeated.

'Well, if you fancy a drink – just me, no groupies – meet me at Yellow at eight. You know it?'

'Yes,' I said, trying not to sound surprised at his choice. Yellow was a trendy and expensive wine bar quite near to my house, frequented by City slickers and C-list celebrities. I'd never actually been inside, but I couldn't imagine Danny there. 'Yes, I'll meet you.'

He grinned. 'Guess I'll see you there, then, Naomi.'

With that, he turned and was gone. I stood motionless

for a second, trying to compose myself. I wanted to jump up and down and scream. Then I ran up the stairs, my body suddenly so weightless that it felt as if my legs were floating above each step.

Emily was waiting for me outside. She was grumpy. 'Where have you been?' she demanded.

'You're not going to believe it, Em!' I was as excited as a small child, my voice high-pitched and breathless. 'I've got a date. With Danny!'

'Oh my God! That's fantastic!' She grasped my hand and beamed at me. 'Oh my God!' Suddenly, the smile vanished and she looked crestfallen. 'But I never even got to meet him.'

Chapter 4

anny was late. Twenty minutes late. I didn't know then that it was his trademark. Our relationship was still a blank slate, like a brand new diary on January First, clean and smelling of freshly milled paper. And, like every new diary, within months it would become a mess of torn edges, smudged writing and scratchings out, its pages filled with adventures and secrets not yet imagined. Beginnings are always perfect: ripe to be spoiled.

I, of course, was ten minutes early. I'd left myself far too long to get ready and had found myself sitting on my bed with nothing to do but stare at my bedside clock and end-lessly re-powder my nose in a vain attempt to quell my nerves. What had made it worse was that my parents were downstairs, circling like sharks. They were after information. It was my fault – I hadn't told them where I was going. It wasn't because I thought they would disapprove, or because I was afraid that they would try to stop me, I simply wasn't ready to divulge anything about Danny. Talking about him would bestow the date with a significance it hadn't yet earned. What if the evening turned out to be a disaster? I'd want to keep the details to myself.

Typically, Dad wouldn't let it drop. He was a born worrier – Mum sometimes called him 'an old woman'. He couldn't rest until he was sure he knew every detail of every-body's schedule. It irritated all of us.

'I'm eighteen,' I'd said earlier, when he'd pressed me. 'I could be at university now, in another city, and you wouldn't have a clue what I was doing. I'm sure Debbie doesn't ring her parents every Friday night to give them a breakdown of her evening ahead.'

He couldn't argue with my logic, but he didn't like it. 'But you're not at university, Naomi,' he had argued. 'You're still at home, living under our roof – and we want to know who you're with and that you're safe.'

'I'll be safe,' I'd promised. 'Just trust me, for once.'

'It's not you we don't trust,' Dad had said, perhaps visu-alising a world full of con men, rapists and murderers out to hurt or maim his daughter.

'Then trust me to use my judgement,' I'd barked. 'I'm not stupid.'

So, at seven-forty, I'd run downstairs, shouted goodbye through the living-room door and let myself out before Dad could start questioning me again. Now I was sitting at Yellow's bar, wondering if Danny would show. It wasn't a bad place to wait alone; Yellow's patrons were too trendy and self-obsessed to hit on a single girl they didn't know, and I had plenty to read. All the day's newspapers were piled up in front of me and there was an extensive wine list and food menu to peruse. My stomach growled as I con-templated the merits of a Thai curry or a goat's cheese salad. I hadn't eaten dinner at home – I was too nervous and I didn't want my tummy to look bloated. My black pencil skirt was far too tight already. And, if I'm honest, I was hopeful that Danny would ask me to eat with him later. The food at Yellow was supposed to be good, if rather over-priced. Would he want to pay or would we go Dutch? Would he stay for just one drink, then tell me he had to leave? What would we talk about? Would I bore him? Would he, for that matter, turn up at all?

For God's sake, chill out, Naomi, I said to myself. *He's been chasing you since you met – why would he suddenly go off you?* I wished I could reach into my brain and stop the cogs from grinding round and round. I ordered a glass of wine and a bowl of olives to keep my hunger pangs at bay. As I popped a couple into my mouth I realised they were marinated in a dressing that tasted strongly of garlic. *Great start, Naomi,* I thought. I rummaged for a mint in my bag. It was covered in fluff, but it would have to do. I swirled it between my teeth until it dissolved, then took a swig of wine. The combination tasted foul.

'Can I get you anything else?' asked the barman politely. It was now ten past eight and I was beginning to look con-spicuous, perched on my bar stool, silent and alone. People don't go to Yellow on their own, they go in big, air-kissing groups.

'No thanks, I'm just waiting for someone.'

The barman smiled. *Poor love,* I read in his eyes. *Have you been stood up?*

I'll give Danny five more minutes, I thought. *Or maybe ten . . .*

When Danny walked in, I didn't notice him. I'd given up on the menu and was now thumbing through a newspaper, devouring a kiss-and-tell story about some footballer. Dad only got the *Financial Times* at home, so reading the tabloids felt like a guilty pleasure.

'Has he been at it again, then?' said Danny dryly, over my shoulder. Flustered, I dropped the paper on to the bar, losing the middle section beneath my stool. Danny bent down to pick it up, pausing a little longer than was necessary as he took in my patterned tights and kitten heels. Smiling cheekily, he handed it back to me. 'Hello, Naomi,' he said. 'Sorry I'm late. Have you been here long?'

'No,' I lied. 'It's fine.' Sitting on the bar stool lent me almost an extra foot and my face was at the same level as his. He looked amazing. His hair was freshly washed and less messy than I'd seen it, curling gently into the nape of his neck. He'd obviously just shaved and, for the first time, I noticed a cute dimple in his chin.

He leaned in towards me and kissed me on the cheek. His musky scent and the warmth of his breath on my neck made me tingle. Then he smiled again and delicately touched my top lip with his thumb and forefinger. The intimacy of this gesture made me feel uncomfortable, until I realised he had merely removed a piece of fluff, which had stuck to my lip-gloss. Seeing me blush, he chose not to comment on it. Evidently, he was a gentleman.

'What are you drinking?' he asked, picking up my wine glass and taking a sip. 'Mmm, I'll order a bottle, shall I?'

I nodded. Danny's confident manner made me feel shy

and nervous, and I worried that if I spoke I might say something stupid.

'Hey, John,' he called out. The barman came over. He winked at Danny, then glanced at me with renewed respect. So Danny was a regular, then? It still seemed incongruous.

'All right, Danny, mate. What can I do for you?'

'Can I have a bottle of Pinot Grigio, please?' he asked. I could have sworn that the posh element of his curious, hybrid accent became a trifle more pronounced. 'Put it on my tab.'

I hadn't expected Danny to know about wine – it didn't fit in with his scruffy, rock-and-roll image. I'd simply ordered one of the few wines that came by the glass in Yellow.

'Why don't we go and sit somewhere more comfortable?' Danny asked when the wine had been brought over. He held out his hand to help me off the stool. I took it, shyly, aware that the feel of his skin on mine was making my heart beat faster and that sparks of electricity were shooting up my arm and into my body. I was conscious too that my own hand was clammy and that I wasn't able to pull down my skirt. Danny didn't appear to notice. He led me through the bar to a table and some plush brown sofas, only letting go of my hand when I sat down. The cushions were softer than I'd expected and I fell back into the sofa, jarring my back. He waited until I'd rearranged my clothes, then sat himself down next to me. His leg touched mine, expectantly.

'That's better,' he said.

'Yes, thanks,' I replied, unsure what to say next, and terribly aware of the proximity of Danny's leg. I hoped he couldn't tell that my legs were trembling. *Think, Naomi, think*, I repeated to myself like a mantra. 'The gig was good,' I volunteered. 'You were good.'

'I'm glad you liked it,' he said. 'We were trying out some new material. It seemed to go down all right.' There was an awkward pause. 'Anyway, enough about me. Tell me about you, Naomi.'

My insecurities came flooding back. I was no good at small talk and, it now transpired, neither was he. His question highlighted the fact that he knew nothing about me, nothing at all. He was out with me because he liked the way I looked, because I'd dared to turn up to his gig and said I liked his music. What was there about me that would interest him?

'What do you want to know?' I managed, buying myself time to think. Danny's motive was genuine – to get to know me – but his question had made me feel self-conscious, anxious that my personality would be scrutinised for flaws. Whatever I said now might make or break our potential relationship.

'I want to know everything.' He laughed, leaning in towards me. 'The name, I've got. How old are you? What's your shoe size? What music do you like – apart from mine, of course? What do you care about? What do you dream about? What do you want to be?'

'OK,' I said, taking a deep breath. 'Stop me when I bore you. My full name – which you don't know – is Naomi Jessica Waterman. I'm eighteen, I have one sister – whom you've seen – called Emily. She's sixteen going on twenty-five. My shoe size is a very average five; I'm five foot five and,' I paused for breath, deciding not to draw attention to my figure by giving him my dress size, 'and I like good music: pop, soul, folk, R & B, indie, jazz, classical, country – anything, so long as it's good. My mum's a music teacher, so we've got about a million CDs at home. She says there are only two types of music: good music and bad music. I have to say I agree with her on that one.'

Danny smiled. He had been nodding, approvingly, throughout my monologue. 'You mum sounds like a very wise woman. Continue.'

Excellent. I'd won a few brownie points. My confidence was growing and I even managed to smile back at him. 'All right. What was your next question? What do I care about? I care about people, my family, my friends, people I don't know. I care about not hurting anyone. I care about animals – I'm vegetarian. I care about the environment. Yes, I know, I sound like a cliché now.' I looked at Danny, expecting him to have grown tired of my rambling. He was concentrating intently, his turquoise eyes wide and piercing.

'Go on . . .'

'I dream about the most bizarre things. Doesn't everyone? I dream about places I've never been, where I meet people I don't know. I dream about being on ships, at fairgrounds, things I've read about or seen in films. I dream in colour, usually, and nearly every night. Sometimes I dream about shoes. Shallow, I know, but I am a girl.'

He laughed again. Now I was starting to relax and enjoy myself.

'What do I want to be? That's a tough one. I thought I wanted to be a lawyer, but now I think that's just what my parents want me to be. I'm on my gap year, working for a law firm and I'm hating every minute of it. All I know is that I want to be somebody, to do something special and important, something that people remember me for. Not tabloid famous – history book famous. God, now I sound like some kind of megalomaniac. Please make me stop before you have to get the men in white coats to carry me out!'

'They'll be coming for me too, then,' he said, suddenly serious. 'I want everything you want. The fame, the glory – plus a bit of adulation too. Of course, when I'm a famous rock star the tabloids will be full of me, but that's part of the job these days, I'm afraid.'

'From what I saw you already have the adulation,' I teased. 'All those girls at The Bunker?'

'No.' He frowned. 'Not the groupies. They only care what I look like and they want to tell their mates they've met me, just in case I make it. I could stand on stage and howl like a wolf and they'd still tell me I was wonderful . . . until the next band comes along. I want respect, I want people to quote my lyrics, I want people to play my records in years to come. Oh God, now who sounds like a megalomaniac?'

'No,' I reassured him. I was smiling automatically now, liking Danny more and more. 'It's good to be ambitious. I hate people who are apathetic and don't have any passion.' I felt a twinge of guilt – wasn't that just how I had been behaving lately? I pushed it away and continued. 'That's what's wrong with my dad. He's so happy being mediocre, going to work every day, like just another ant.'

'Sounds like my dad,' said Danny. 'Except he's got all the ants working for him. Pardon the mixed metaphor, but he's the big cheese: Mr John Evans, MBE, head of Evans Inc, purveyor of plastics to the world.'

'Wow,' I said, 'I'm impressed. He sounds important.' So that was where the posh vowels in Danny's voice came from! Nobody in my family had letters after their name. The more I found out about Danny, the more of a mystery he became.

Danny shrugged. 'Don't be. He's not important to me.' He voice sounded flat and his body seemed to crumple inwards. The sparkle in his eyes had dimmed noticeably. It made me feel uncomfortable, like I'd intruded on something private.

'Hey,' I said, brightly, trying to lift his spirits. 'You know loads about me now. What about you, Danny Evans?'

'Daniel, ahem, Hector, ahem, Evans,' he said, with a mock-bashful look. I decided it was all right to laugh.

'I know, I know,' he sighed. 'I was named after my grandfather. That's how people with bad names get back at the world – they pass them on to their descendants. It's a cruel trick.'

'It could have been worse,' I ventured.

'Not much,' he said.

'Actually, you might be right,' I teased.

'Enough now,' said Danny, playfully slapping my leg. I felt the jolt of electricity again and found myself wishing he would leave his hand there. 'You don't know me well enough to take the piss.'

The funny thing is, I felt like I did. We'd only been chatting for fifteen minutes or so, yet it seemed as if I'd known him for years. I'd never felt so comfortable, so quickly, with anybody. With Danny I could be one hundred per cent myself.

Apparently fearing he'd offended me, he qualified his remark. 'Yet,' he stated.

'Does that mean you're planning to stick around?' I asked, surprised at my boldness.

'Absolutely, Naomi. I'm not going anywhere. Are you?'

The next hour passed in an instant. I was never any good at physics at school, but things like time travel and black holes in space have always made a kind of sense to me. Time is a strange concept – it's divided neatly into seconds, minutes and hours, but they're purely artificial; they don't really mean anything. A few minutes can seem like an eternity when you're a small child desperate to arrive at your destination, and likewise when you're grown up and unhappy or in pain. But whole hours can vanish inexplicably when you're immersed in conversation, drunk or enjoying yourself. When old people say they don't know where the years have gone, I genuinely understand what they mean.

I learned that Danny was twenty and an only child. He had gone to Oxford straight after A-levels to study English literature, but had dropped out, disillusioned, at the end of his first year. Presently, he was concentrating on The Wonderfulls, determined to make his band a success. He had done odd jobs for pocket money – waiting at tables, a stint behind a bar and in a record shop. Now that The Wonderfulls were regularly playing paid gigs he spent most of the week rehearsing and recording in the studio he'd built in the basement of his parents' house. His mother, an ex-model, filled her time organising charity functions and lunching with her friends. She left him to his own devices. He said she was cold and distant – like an icy blonde in a Hitchcock film. I didn't dare to ask about his father again.

'Do you fancy some food?' he asked, when I came back from a visit to the Ladies and there was a natural lull in our conversation. It was a quarter to ten and I was starting to feel weak and dizzy. While it's true that I hadn't eaten for hours and my empty stomach was now swimming in alcohol, I can't deny that my giddiness was in no small part due to the sheer adrenaline rush of being with Danny.

'Yes,' I said, with rather more enthusiasm than I'd intended. 'I'm starving. They do food here, don't they?'

'They do, but I know somewhere much nicer. Trust me.'

'OK.' I smiled as he helped me put on my coat. I was all thumbs and elbows and, once again, his touch made me quiver. He stroked the fake fur collar, smoothing down the pile with the palm of his hand. 'Nice coat.'

'Thanks. I got it in a vintage shop. It's from the 1950s, I think.'

'You have great style, Naomi. Very individual. That's just one of the many things I'm beginning to like about you.'

He linked his arm through mine and took me to an Italian restaurant about half a mile up the road. La Casa Nostra was newly opened – it still smelled of fresh paint – and I'd read about in the newspaper. Its proprietor was an ex-footballer and it attracted the local celebrity crowd, those who didn't want to make the trip into central London. People went there to be seen, rather than to eat – although the chef was supposed to be excellent. It was the last place I had expected Danny to take me. Like Yellow, it didn't fit with his scruffy, musician's persona. I wondered if he was trying to impress me or whether this was the sort of place he went to all the time. And how could he afford it? Even regular gigs and stints behind a bar couldn't bring in that much.

I'd never have gone there without him; just walking through the front door was an intimidating experience. Even though I was 'nicely' brought up, posh, trendy restaurants make me feel insecure and clumsy. I don't know which cutlery to use or when to thank the waiter.

Danny must have noticed the anxiety in my face. 'Don't worry,' he said. 'They're really nice in here. I used to work in a pub with the guy behind the bar – he'll see you're all right.'

We were shown to a small table by the window, decorated with a thin glass vase containing a single orchid. As the waiter pulled out my chair he discreetly removed a 'Reserved' sign from the table. Danny saw that I'd noticed and smiled. 'I hope you don't mind. I was optimistic about tonight.'

'How did you know we'd get on?' I asked.

'I just knew,' he said, looking directly into my eyes with an intensity that seemed almost like sadness. 'There was something about you. Even on the bus, I just knew.'

I stared back at him, speechless. If anyone else had given

me this line, I'd have laughed at loud. But it wasn't corny when Danny said it because *I* knew too – because I felt exactly the same.

Even if I'd known how to respond, I didn't get the chance – the waiter arrived to take our order. When we received our meals, the portions were small, but the food was delicious. We each had a taste of one another's courses and Danny bemoaned the fact he hadn't ordered the same pasta dish as me – with asparagus, wild mushrooms and a saffron sauce. He insisted that we both have dessert, daring me not to agree that the chocolate mousse was the best I'd ever tasted.

'You win,' I conceded, as the last spoonful of creamy sweetness melted on my tongue.

'In that case,' he teased, his eyes twinkling, 'I get to choose my prize.'

'Yes . . . ?'

'Um,' he said, scratching his head comically. 'Let's see. I know . . . you let me take you out again.'

'What a cruel and unusual punishment!' I cried, playing along. 'OK, but I must let you know how painful it will be for me.'

'I know exactly how to torture a woman,' he said in a terrible imitation of a German accent. He laughed at himself. 'How about Sunday? Sunday daytime. I know just the place. But I'm not going to tell you where yet. You'd better give me your number so I can text you tomorrow . . . in code, of course.'

'I'm definitely free on Sunday,' I said. 'You're making it sound very mysterious, Mr Evans.'

He took out a chewed-up biro from his inside jacket pocket and handed it to me. 'Your number?' he asked. I rummaged inside my bag and found an old receipt, turned it over and wrote my details on the plain side. When I passed it to Danny he studied it intently, as if he was committing the digits to memory, before putting it away.

'Tell me,' I asked, 'What would you have done if you'd lost the bet?'

'I never lose,' he said, his tone unexpectedly serious. Then he winked and I laughed, but I still wasn't convinced that he'd said it in jest.

By the time the waiter had cleared away our coffee cups and brought the bill it was well after midnight. Danny insisted on paying, which was fortunate, as it came to almost my week's salary. *How can he afford it?* I asked myself, for the second time that evening. *I must not get used to living like this*, I noted. *Next year I'll be a student living on baked beans and pot noodles.*

As we were handed our coats I wondered what Danny had planned for Sunday – the excitement was rising within me and I didn't know how I'd get through the next day. Only a few hours before, Danny had been a virtual stranger. Now I couldn't imagine a full thirty-six hours without him. See, time *is* a crazy concept, isn't it?

Danny walked me home, slowly, with his arm draped around my shoulders. The difference in our heights meant that I fitted neatly into his side and I felt safe, as if I belonged there. Whenever we stopped to cross a road he'd take my hand, sliding each of his fingers between mine.

Every time he did it I felt my cheeks flush and I hoped that in the darkness he couldn't tell. We talked all the way, learning more about each other's CD collections and swapping stories about our travels. I'd never been further than Europe, but Danny told me he'd spent the previous summer travelling in Sri Lanka with a friend. He said it was the most beautiful place on earth and the people were the most friendly and hospitable he'd ever met. He'd promised himself he would go back one day, but first there were many other places to see, like Thailand, Australia and India.

He described his pride and joy to me: a Fender Telecaster guitar, which he'd received as an eighteenth birthday present. Just thinking about it made him animated. He was like a small child – bright-eyed and breathless – unselfconsciously imagining it in his arms and stroking it as if it were a treasured pet. His enthusiasm for it was so sweet, so infectious, that I had an urge to stop and hug him, right there in the middle of the street.

We were already beginning to create our own shared language, our own in-jokes. It seemed to happen organically. At some point in the evening, I don't remember when, he had re-christened me Omi and then I became Omi Wan Kenobi, after the character in *Star Wars*. On cue, I'd done my finest Alec Guinness impression, reciting, 'May the Force be with you.' Although I didn't particularly like the moniker, I loved the fact that Danny had given it to me. We laughed about a woman in the restaurant whose skirt was so tight that she could barely sit down. Danny did an impression of her struggling into her chair and then I, rather more used to negotiating clingy skirts and high heels, showed him how to do it properly.

All the way home I was aware of what was coming: the inevitable kiss, our first kiss. The anticipation was almost unbearable and at the same time, intensely pleasurable. Each time he touched my fingers, dwarfing my hand in his, I felt electric currents course throughout my body. I wanted the kiss to happen and I wanted it to be over. It hung over me like a cloud heavy with nerves; a good kiss would be a flawless ending to a wonderful evening, a clumsy one might spoil it all.

'This is me, then,' I said, hesitantly, as we arrived at my garden gate. My pulse was thundering in my ears and my teeth were chattering, even though I wasn't cold. All the lights in my house were off and, in the poor lamp light, I could barely see Danny's face. We stood silently for a second, looking at each other and then Danny took both my hands in his. I could feel him trembling too.

'Goodnight, Omi,' he said, softly. 'Thank you for a lovely evening.' Gently dropping my hands, he leaned towards me, placing his arms around me and drawing me into his body. He was so much taller than me that he had to stoop, and I instinctively cradled his face in my palms. And then he kissed me, tenderly at first, then more passionately. His lips were soft and full, his tongue warm and strong. I felt feather-light, as if my feet were hovering above the ground. It was the perfect kiss.

If only things could have remained that perfect. If only time could have stopped and Danny and I could still be standing outside my front door in the darkness, holding each other. If I could climb into a time machine right now, I'd go back to that moment. And stay there, forever.

Chapter 5

When Danny had disappeared up my street (he looked back twice – I counted, naturally), and the sensation of his kiss had faded from my lips, I realised there was nothing for it but to resume normality and go into my house. Assuming everybody was asleep, I turned my key in the lock as quietly as I could and closed the front door behind me with a gentle push.

I didn't want to go straight to bed, so I went into the living room and curled up on the sofa, arranging the cushions around my body like a cocoon. I wasn't really sure what I was doing there, or how long I'd stay, but it didn't seem right to end *this* day like any other, and I wasn't tired. In fact, I was wide awake with excitement. I went over and over the date in my mind, replaying every word of every conversation, every look and every touch. I felt the urge to write it all down, but thought better of it. It seemed too contrived. I didn't keep a diary; I'd tried several times when I was younger, always finding it too much effort to maintain for more than a few weeks.

I must have fallen asleep where I sat because when I next looked at my watch it was three a.m., I was cold and could feel a pull in my neck. 'Time for bed, Naomi,' I said, aloud, as I dragged my unwilling body up from the soft cushions. I stumbled on the stairs, going over on my ankle and banging my hand on the wooden banister as I tried to steady myself. I decided against going into the bathroom to take off my make-up and clean my teeth. It was too much effort and the sensation of water on my face would only wake me up. *One night won't hurt*, I told myself. A wise and sensible voice in my head said, *You'll only have yourself to blame if you wake up tomorrow with an enormous zit.* I chose to ignore it.

I opened my bedroom door, pulled off my clothes and left them where they fell. I intended to climb straight into bed, but then something – the half-conscious awareness of a presence in the room – made me jump. More alert now, with my eyes adjusting to the darkness, I could make out a silhouette, a figure, on my bed. For a brief moment I thought – or was it wished? – it might be Danny. Perhaps, not wanting our date to end, he had climbed in through my window and waited for me. But just as quickly, I knew the thought was ridiculous, the type of thing that only happens in books and films, and something which, in truth, would have terrified me. Of course, it could only be Emily.

She looked so peaceful, all curled up, with her fine hair fanned out on my pillow, that I didn't want to wake her. I thought about going to sleep in her room instead. But then she stirred and became aware that I was leaning over her. 'Nay?' she croaked, making an effort to sit up. Sleep still had a hold of her body and her coordination, and so she crumpled back down again.

'It's all right, Em,' I said softly. 'I'm home now. What are you doing here, on my bed? You silly thing – you're lucky I didn't squash you.'

My words jolted her awake. 'God, Nay,' she said, this time managing to prop herself up. 'Where have you been? I was so worried about you when you didn't call me, and I rang you so many times and you didn't pick up!'

Oh hell, now it was coming back to me. I'd promised Emily I'd go to the loo and ring her halfway through the date, to let her know I was OK and that Danny hadn't turned out to be some sort of weirdo. I was also supposed to tell her if I was bored and wanted her to call me and give me a random reason to leave – an escape plan. We'd even agreed on a code word, in case I couldn't find anywhere private. All I'd needed to say was, 'Is Simon over the chickenpox yet?' and she'd call back a few minutes later with a fictional emergency so pressing that I would have no option but to leave. How could I have forgotten? Because I was having such a great time with Danny, that's how.

'Oh Em, I'm so sorry. I just didn't think. I didn't need to call you and I didn't know you were trying to get hold of me.'

'It's all right. It's just that you're normally so reliable that I thought something must be up. So it was good, then? The date?'

I found myself smiling. 'Yes, it was amazing.'

'Really?' she gushed. 'Tell me all about it, right now. Every detail.'

Pleased to have an enthusiastic audience, I told Emily everything about the date, from the garlicky olives to the goodnight kiss. She 'oohed' and 'aahed' in all the right places, interrupting me to ask what I thought were trivial questions about which celebrities were in Yellow (none that I'd noticed), and whether I'd told Danny much about her (I lied and said he had asked when he could meet her properly). She also asked for rather more detail about the kiss than was strictly necessary. 'Pur-lease, Em,' I said when she began to get far too technical. 'If you want kissing tips, go and read a magazine.'

'Don't get all high and mighty with me,' she retorted, obviously embarrassed. 'I've kissed more boys than you.'

'Maybe so,' I conceded. 'But quality is more important than quantity, isn't it?'

'Charming!' she huffed, pouting at me. She yawned and stretched, then brought her arm round to her face and tried to make out the time from the dim fluorescent display on her watch. 'Blimey, Nay, it's four in the morning. I've got work tomorrow.'

'Sorry, Emily,' I said. 'Go to bed now. And thanks again.' I gave her a little hug, just like I'd done when she was little and had fallen over in the playground at our primary school, or one of the older girls had tried to bully her. We hadn't hugged for years – not since she was ten or eleven. After that, she'd seemed so disdainful of any physical contact with me. Now, she didn't seem to mind at all.

I slept fitfully, waking every hour or so. Consciousness brought with it the memory of the kiss. I'd lie in the dark, imagining Danny was kissing me again, giving myself but-terflies and smiling until I could no longer keep my eyes open. When I finally awoke fully, it was midday. I could hear my parents moving about downstairs, murmuring to each other. They were probably discussing me, wondering when it would be late enough to come upstairs and drag me out of bed so they could grill me about my date. My ally, Emily, had long since gone out to her Saturday job. I would have to deal with them alone.

My clothes were scattered all over the bedroom floor. I stepped over them and went into the bathroom. When I peered into the mirror, the person who looked back was barely recognisable. She had hair the same colour as mine – chestnut brown with auburn streaks – but it was knotted and matted to her head on one side, frizzing over her shoulders on the other. Her eyes, like mine, were green, but they were puffy and half-closed, the lashes glued together with clumps of black mascara, which had also worked its way down her cheeks. Her nose was red, blotchy and shiny and her lips chapped and flaking. Looking at her appalled me.

After a shower, I felt more myself again. I made my way to the kitchen and poured myself a full pint of water from the tap, downing it in three gulps. My throat was dry and scratchy, like it is at the beginning of a cold. *All I need now is to get ill*, I thought to myself. *I've got to be on top form tomorrow. For Danny.* Just thinking his name made me smile.

Mum came into the kitchen and caught me grinning to myself. 'Good night?' she asked.

'Yes, thanks,' I said, unable to remove the smile.

'It must have been. You normally say, "It was all right," wherever you've been. So who is he? Emily said he was someone you met at work. Is he doing articles at the firm?'

So my parents had been fishing for information, then. Poor Emily. I had to admire her quick thinking – the story she'd come up with would surely have pleased Dad.

'What? Oh, no, Emily must have got confused. That's someone else.' There was no point perpetuating the lie. Now that I was to see Danny again – and hopefully not just the once – it would become too confusing in the long run. 'He's actually a musician.'

'Oh?' Mum was delighted. 'What does he play?'

'He's in the band I went to see the other night. He plays guitar and he sings. He's really good.'

'Who's good?' said Dad, appearing through the kitchen door. He made an exaggerated point of looking at his watch and then at me. 'Good morning!' he announced, sarcastically. 'So you're finally awake, then. Did you have a good night?'

'She did,' said Mum, smiling at me. I had her on side. 'She had a date with a musician.'

Dad looked perplexed for a moment. I could tell from the knot in his forehead that he was wondering whether the women in his house had once again conspired to keep him in the dark. 'Oh. And how old is he, this musician?'

'He's twenty,' I said, aware that my parents would consider this an acceptable age gap, since there were two years between them too.

'And what's his name?'

'He's called Danny. Danny Evans.' Knowing that Dad would be impressed by Danny's background, I continued: 'I think his dad is some sort of businessman. Plastics, or something. He's an MBE.'

'Ah,' said Dad, the tone of his voice changing from concerned to proud. 'John Evans. I know him. Very important man, gives a lot to charity. You know, Martha – he belongs to the Rotary club.'

Mum nodded, with disinterest. I had no doubt that she would rather hear about Danny's music.

'Well, well,' said Dad. 'So you're going out with John Evans's son.'

I didn't feel I should tell him that Danny didn't like his father – appeared to hate him even.

'So when do we get to meet this Danny, then?'

'Leave her alone, David,' Mum said, in the same voice she used to tell me and Emily off. 'She's only been on one date. I'm sure she'll let us meet him when she's ready.'

'Sure,' I said, already dreading that day. 'I don't want to scare him off. Maybe in a few weeks.'

Unlike Dad, Mum knew it was time for the cross-examination to end. 'Naomi, your dad and I are going into town to do some shopping. You're welcome to join us.'

'No thanks,' I said. 'I've got a few things to do myself.'

I had nothing to do, of course – just an afternoon to fill while I waited for Danny to text me about tomorrow's date. When my parents had left I went back up to my bedroom and tidied away my clothes. It took no time at all. After that, I decided to call Debbie, to tell her how the date had gone. I was a little disappointed that she hadn't called me first. I'd rung and told her how much I liked Danny and she knew it was my first date for many months. Wasn't she interested? I hoped that wasn't the case.

I couldn't find my phone and panicked, momentarily, until I remembered I'd left it in my coat pocket. The coat – which Danny had so admired – was hanging over the banister at the bottom of the stairs. *It is a beautiful coat*, I thought, stroking the collar, just as he had done. I was sure I could still make out the faint smell of his aftershave, or was that just dry-cleaning fluid?

I took out my phone and saw that it was switched off, just as Emily had said. I couldn't remember doing that. As soon as I switched it on it bleeped and shuddered violently; I had twenty missed calls and four messages – all from Emily. It was nice that she had been so concerned and, for the second time, I felt guilty that I hadn't called her. I played each message through before deleting it. Emily had started off with a cool, 'Hi, Nay, hope you're enjoying your date,' (giggle). 'Let me know who's in Yellow tonight'; progressing to a concerned, 'Are you all right, Nay? Please give me a call'; to 'Naomi – call me!'. Her last message was, 'I'm hoping you're OK, Naomi. I'm going to wait up for you.'

Debbie hadn't called once.

The phone rang about six times before Debbie picked up.

'Hi, Naomi,' she said. 'I was going to call you this afternoon. What are you up to?'

'Nothing much,' I said, annoyed that she appeared to have forgotten about my date. 'What about you?'

'I've got an essay to write. I should have done it last week, but you know what it's like.'

'What's it on?' I asked. I didn't care a jot, but it seemed the polite question.

'Something to do with the causes of the First World War. Pretty dull stuff. I'm hoping to get it done today because a group of us are going to head out on a trip tomorrow. Mike, the guy I told you about who lives in my halls, is driving us.'

'That's nice,' I said. I no longer felt like telling her about Danny and I wanted the conversation to be over as quickly as possible.

'So what's been happening with you? Oh yes, have you gone out with that guy yet?'

So she did remember.

'Yes, it was last night.'

'And?'

'And it was great. We had a really good time and I'm seeing him again tomorrow.' I left out all the detail because I could tell she didn't have time to hear it. The evening deserved to be more than an anecdote; I had hoped to give her a minute-by-minute account, so she'd be as excited about Danny as me.

'Are you upset with me, Naomi?' she asked, meekly. She knew it wasn't like me to be so concise.

'No,' I half-lied. I was upset, but I knew it wasn't entirely her fault. If only she wasn't so far away, then we could talk for hours, like we used to.

'Oh. You just don't sound like you, that's all.'

'Must be a bad line,' I said. 'Listen, I'd better go – I've

got to go and meet Emily. I'll call you tomorrow, after my date.'

'Please do!' she said, her voice rising an octave or two. She was trying to make up for her previous lack of enthusiasm. 'Actually, no, I'll call you – when we get back from our trip.'

'All right, then,' I said. 'Speak to you then.'

I put the phone down before she could finish saying goodbye. Was this what our friendship was going to be like from now on – snatched exchanges of headlines with no details? Then I had a little cry and decided to do the only thing that would cheer me up: I went shopping.

I was in the Topshop changing room, working my way through a pile of chocolate brown and khaki trousers, when my phone rang. Call me psychic, but I knew it was Danny before I saw his name come up on the screen. I had the butterflies to prove it.

'Naomi,' he said. I could only just hear him over the din of the music. 'How are you?' The intimacy we had shared the night before was gone and I was conscious once again of the odd inflections in his hybrid accent. We were strangers again, polite and nervous strangers.

'I'm good, thanks. How are you? Did you get home OK?'

'I'm good, yes, no hassle. Where are you? It's the middle of the afternoon, but if I didn't know better, I'd swear you'd gone clubbing.'

'You're almost right,' I said, laughing. 'I'm in Topshop.'

'Do you want to go outside? I can hardly hear you.'

Loving Danny

'Um, yes, wait a minute.' I couldn't move. My trousers were round my ankles, my shoes buried under the reject-trouser pile. 'Actually, Danny, can I call you back in a few minutes? I'm in the changing room and I, er, need to get dressed first.'

'Oh, OK.' He sounded embarrassed. He wasn't the only one. 'Sorry.'

'I'll be literally two minutes, I promise.'

I pulled on my jeans and shoes as quickly as I could and rushed out of the changing room, handing a messy pile of trousers to the shop assistant. I hadn't put them back on their hangers and she tutted as I walked away. *Serves you right*, I thought, *for being so unhelpful when I asked for a different size.*

Once I was outside the store I paused to catch my breath. The high street was heaving with Saturday shoppers, and the roar of the traffic, with buses lined up end to end, was almost as loud as the music I'd escaped. I headed down a side street and found a small café with tables outside. Sitting myself down, I called Danny, using the 'Last Call Received' option. I wondered how long it would be before I knew his number off by heart. Would it be presumptuous of me – tempting fate – to put it on speed dial?

He picked up immediately. 'Hi there, I was beginning to think you'd changed your mind,' he said. 'Or are you wearing your entire wardrobe today?'

'I had to change into my Wonder Woman costume,' I joked. 'I'm out of practice. No, I thought I'd find somewhere I could actually hear you.'

'Good. Well, you know why I'm calling. It's about tomorrow.'

I felt a little sick. He wasn't going to cancel me, was he? Had he had second thoughts about me? 'Yes? Is it still all right? Weren't you going to text me?'

'I was,' he said. 'Well remembered. But I couldn't think of a clever enough code, so I gave up and thought I'd give you a call instead. I apologise.'

'Some spy you'd make, double-O Evans.' I cringed at my terrible joke. He kindly ignored it.

'So, if you still want to see me again, here's the plan. Meet me by the pond in King Edward's park at two p.m. And wear your Wonder Woman costume.'

'It's got to go to the dry cleaner's, I'm afraid. But two in the park sounds good. I'm intrigued. Are we going to feed the ducks?'

'Maybe,' he said. 'Maybe not. Enough questions – you'll have to wait and see. I'm looking forward to it.'

'Me too.' He had no idea how much. 'Bye, Danny. Take care.'

'Bye, Omi.'

And with a click, he was gone.

I went to bed early that night, but I couldn't sleep. Lying in so late and doing very little all day had left me with an excess of energy and no outlet for it. I tried to read for a while, but the words danced before my eyes. After scanning the same page three times, and absorbing none of it, I gave up. The truth was that I wasn't interested in the lives of the characters in the novel. I only wanted to know about Danny, to discover what the next day, the next chapter in *our* story, would bring.

Even then, I had an instinct that our burgeoning relationship was to be an important one for me, something that would mark and change me, that I would talk about in years to come. I'd had two 'serious' boyfriends before I met Danny, the first at fifteen and the second from sixteen to seventeen. I had cared for them both, but I had never really loved either of them, at least not in the way I believed love should feel. Both relationships had developed out of friendship, jogging along sweetly until I grew bored and felt it was kinder to put an end to things.

Mark, the boy who had made me the compilation CD, was the son of my parents' friends. We'd grown up together, spending summer Sunday afternoons at barbecues and evenings at each other's houses, ordered to play upstairs while our parents hosted dinner parties. By the time we'd turned fifteen, getting together seemed like the obvious thing to do; it would almost have been rude not to. It was the lazy option, so much easier for both of us than meeting a stranger at a party or youth club and enduring weeks of uncertainty, coded looks and gossip. To me, Mark represented familiarity and safety. We could practise kissing and fumbling with each other without any risk of getting hurt, or anybody else finding out.

The trouble was, I don't think I ever really fancied Mark – I thought of him as a mate and I assumed he felt the same way. It turned out that I was very wrong. When I broke up with him, one hot Tuesday afternoon in the summer holidays after our GCSEs (not long after he gave me the CD), he cried. He told me he'd thought we'd be together for years and that one day we'd get married. After that, he never spoke to me again.

My second proper relationship was with Jack, a guy who joined my school in the Sixth Form. We took the same classes and often found ourselves working on joint projects. We got together at his house while revising for a test and our relationship lasted the whole school year. I really fancied Jack – he had a mop of blond hair and an athletic build, a bit like David Beckham (though that's exaggerating his handsomeness). He was kind and sexy, but he was too much like hard work. He thought of himself as the strong, silent type – he rarely revealed what he was thinking or feeling and I'd have to drag it out of him. But what he had to say was never interesting enough to merit the effort. When he had his hair cut short, I did the same to our relationship.

Since Jack, there had been nobody special, just a few snogs at parties. I was impatient, ready for 'the real thing', for love and passion and excitement and intensity. And now, there was Danny, with his music and his dark lyrics and his ambition. You could say we were a perfect fit.

Chapter 6

I've never been one for surprises – I don't like being thrown off guard and having to improvise. I always like to be prepared, to be wearing the right clothes and to have my things with me, just in case. What's more, I'm not a good actress – my real emotions are too transparent – and surprises are almost always a disappointment for me. Generally, I end up feeling guilty and the person who has gone to the trouble of surprising me wonders why they bothered.

So, while it was a lovely, romantic idea, Danny's surprise date had me fretting. You know where you are with a bar, restaurant, cinema or club – but a park? At the end of October? I had absolutely no idea what to wear (it might rain or be muddy), how much make-up to put on (bright sunshine can be unforgiving), and whether to shave my legs to the knee or all the way up. I was afraid I would be forced to do something I hated, like rollerblading, or something which might require me to take off my clothes and reveal my pale, untoned body, like swimming (which, I'll admit, was highly unlikely at that time of year). There were simply too many unknown quantities.

In the event, I left all my options open. I wore combats (hard-wearing, comfortable) and a pretty top (for glamour), draped a chunky, wool zip-up cardigan over my shoulders, and I packed my most compact umbrella in my shoulder bag, together with a swimming costume and a small towel – just in case – and my make-up bag. I shaved my legs from ankle to thigh, applied fake tan, waterproof mascara, concealer and long-lasting lipstick. I felt like a soldier, preparing myself for a campaign in a foreign country.

And, like every good soldier, I was on time, arriving at the park at fourteen-hundred hours prompt. Danny was late again – eighteen minutes and twenty three seconds late, if we're being (militarily) precise. On this occasion I had no doubt that he would turn up and I was merely annoyed. It may have been mid-afternoon, but I was alone in a wide open space and I felt vulnerable. I didn't even have anywhere to sit – there were no benches near the pond. It was a grey and sunless day, and I shivered, wishing I'd brought a coat. Still, waiting for Danny again, and now beginning to recognise that he had at least one flaw, made me less nervous about this, our second date.

I saw him before he saw me. He was walking up the path that leads from the main entrance of the park and snakes around its perimeter, branching off in several directions towards the pond or the tennis courts or the cricket pitch. He appeared to be carrying something heavy, which was causing him to stoop and making his progress uneven and slow. I wondered if I should run towards him and offer to help, but I didn't want to spoil his surprise. So I turned the other way and feigned intense interest in a family of swans swimming across the pond. When his footsteps drew close behind me, I pretended not to hear them and tried to stifle the smile that was involuntarily spreading across my face.

'Hello, Naomi,' he said, over my shoulder. He was panting. 'Are you ready for your surprise?'

Not as ready as I was twenty minutes ago, I felt like saying. He hadn't even apologised this time. But when I turned and looked at him, breathless and stiff-armed from carrying what was now obviously an enormous picnic basket, my irritation vanished. 'Absolutely,' I said, allowing him to kiss me on the cheek. The sensation of his lips on my skin again made my heart lurch. I ached for him to kiss me again, properly, like he had two nights before. 'Bring it on.'

'OK, but first you need to trust me. I'm going to blindfold you. Is that all right?'

'Um, yes, OK.' I was nervous and excited at the same time. 'You're not going to push me in the pond, are you?'

'Not my style,' he said, smiling. 'Maybe it was, ten years ago, but no, what I've got planned does not involve dunking you.'

Danny placed his hands on my shoulders and I let him turn me around. Then I felt the caress of smooth fabric – it must have been silk – across my face, slipping over my ears and around the back of my head. He tied it loosely, smoothing down my hair with his palm. 'OK, now take my hand.'

We walked, awkwardly, for a few minutes, the picnic basket bashing into Danny's legs with each step. I humoured him by acting disoriented – it made him grasp my hand more tightly – but I could actually see the grass and the path through the bottom of my blindfold.

'We're here now,' he said, sighing with relief as he put down the picnic basket. 'You can stop.' He untied the blindfold, letting it drop to the floor at my feet. There, in front of me, was one of the most beautiful sights I had ever seen. The park's ancient gazebo had been decorated with multi-coloured flowers and ribbons and tinsel. There were even bunches of grapes hanging from its poles. It looked like something you'd see in an epic movie set in Roman times.

'Oh my God!' I exclaimed. Had Danny really done this just for me? When had he done it? I'd had no idea how thoughtful he was, how inventive. Worried that I might begin to cry, I hugged him, a little too tightly. Then, embarrassed, I pulled away.

'Do you like it?' he asked, trying to gauge my emotions from my perplexing expression.

'What do you think?' I laughed. 'It's beautiful. Thank you.'

Reassured, Danny then opened the enormous picnic basket, taking from it two large, green floor cushions, which he placed side by side within the gazebo. 'Now, if Madame would care to sit,' he suggested, bowing and waving his hand like a courtier. I stepped into the gazebo and sat myself down cross-legged, while he continued to unload the basket. He took from it two plates, two cups and two sets of plastic cutlery, which he spread out on a tartan blanket. Then he brought out the food, the majority of it in tiny portion-sized containers, which I recognised from the posh delicatessen on the high street. He must have spent a fortune. There were giant olives, feta cheese, a pasta salad, stuffed vine leaves, asparagus spears, sun-dried tomato bread, lemon hummus, rocket salad with parmesan shavings, Kettle Chips and honey-roasted almonds. For dessert there was an exotic fruit salad and strawberries dipped in chocolate. It was all my favourite food, everything I'd mentioned liking on our first date. There was even – somewhat incongruously – a bag of dolly mixtures, because I'd told him they were my favourite sweets when I was a child. I was so overwhelmed by his thoughtfulness and attention to detail that I couldn't speak.

'Is everything OK?' asked Danny, looking slightly anxious. 'Or would you rather we'd gone to McDonald's?'

'Very funny,' I said, resisting the urge to hug him again. 'It's gorgeous. Incredible. I just don't know what to say.'

He beamed. 'Don't say anything. Eat.'

As we enjoyed the food, Danny told me about The Wonderfulls' most important gig ever, which would take place in February at the 142 Club in town. 'There's going to be an A & R guy – a talent spotter – there from Excite Records,' he said. 'Word on the street is that they're looking to sign a band like us.'

'Wow,' I said. 'That's amazing.'

'It is, but we're going to have to get a hell of a lot of practice in between now and then.' He saw me looking downcast. 'Oh God, Omi, that didn't come out right. I didn't mean I won't be able to see you again. I want you to be part of it all and, with your extensive musical knowledge, you can give me feedback on some new songs.'

'Really?' I asked. 'Won't the others mind? I don't want to become some sort of Yoko Ono hate figure.'

'No,' he said. 'I'm the songwriter and the lead singer – it's my band, really. Don't worry about it. They're great guys – you'll like them. And they'll love you. As far as I'm concerned, from now on you're permanently on the guest list.'

We smiled coyly at each other, acknowledging that each of us saw a place for the other in our future, but not wanting to spell it out for fear of appearing too forward.

While we'd been in the park the sky had darkened considerably, and the clouds had brought with them an icy, damp wind. I didn't want to put my cardigan on properly because, suddenly self-conscious, I was sure the chunky wool made me look fat. Instead, I draped it over my shoulders and chided myself for not wearing a coat. Danny noticed me shivering. He was only wearing a T-shirt and thin leather jacket, yet he appeared immune to the cold, as men often seem to be. 'I've brought another blanket along,' he said. 'Why don't we wrap it around us?' He clambered up and went over to the basket, pulling out a soft, cream alpaca throw. I raised my eyebrows. If there was one thing I knew about, it was fabrics, and this was no picnic blanket.

'This is my mum's, actually,' Danny explained. 'She'd go mad if she knew I'd brought it, but she never uses it herself. Why waste it, eh?' He sat down next to me and draped the throw over us. It was only then I realised how much I'd been longing for this contact again. He was so close that I could feel the warmth of his body, and the anticipation of another kiss began to grow within me. I would have been happy to sit there with him like that for hours, but, within minutes, it had begun to drizzle, then to rain heavily. Fat droplets of water trickled through the sides of the gazebo, causing the ribbons, which Danny had so artfully arranged, to bleed red, blue and yellow.

'Shit!' he cried, as a globule of yellow water stained the throw. 'We'd better make a run for it! This rain is practically horizontal. There's a shelter over there. I'll come back for the picnic stuff later. Are you ready to go?'

'OK,' I said, picking up my bag and holding my cardigan together at my neck. He grabbed my hand and started running. His legs were so much longer than mine that I was being dragged along, my feet barely touching the ground.

'Stop a second,' he said, laughing at me. 'I've got an idea. Climb on my back.'

He bent over and I jumped on his back, flinging my arms around his neck as he grasped for my legs. I was aware that it was a long time since anybody had given me a piggy-back and, the last time, I'd been rather smaller and lighter. *I hope he doesn't think I'm a heifer*, I thought. As we moved, I was half on, half off, pulling Danny's T-shirt from his shoulder and accidentally kneeing him in the small of his back. Despite my discomfort, the sensation of his strong, muscular body beneath mine was tantalising. We were both giggling hysterically, becoming wetter and wetter and more bedraggled, and no longer caring.

Danny tipped me off his back at the entrance to the shelter. For a minute we just stood there laughing at each other. 'Whose stupid idea was it to have a picnic in October?' he said, raising his eyebrows in self-mockery. 'Now what do we do? We're both dripping wet, the food has gone swimming and I don't think there's much chance of getting served in here.'

We looked around us. The shelter was like a bus stop – a small metal hut with no front and a bench inside – except no buses would ever stop there.

'Hang on,' I said, as a realisation struck me. 'I've got a towel! See?' I pulled the towel from my bag and handed it to Danny. He took it gratefully, rubbing it over the top of his head and then across his face. He looked so cute wet, with his hair sticking out in all directions.

'Here, let me,' he said. He delicately pressed the towel to my face, wiping the droplets of water from my nose and my chin. The feel of his fingers on my face, even through the roughness of the towel, was thrilling and I stifled a sigh. Then he gathered my hair together at the back and wrapped the towel around it like a headdress.

He chuckled. 'Now you look like a nun,' he said. 'Which wasn't really my intention. Anyway, Naomi Waterman – an apt name if ever there was one, today at least – what sort of girl brings a towel on a date?'

'I used to be in the Brownies,' I said. 'You know, always be prepared.'

'I always am,' he said with a cheeky smile, as he moved closer.

What do two people on a second date do, alone in a shelter, while they wait for the rain to stop? They pick up where they left off at the end of the first date, of course. And so, at last, while the rain clattered on the roof, we kissed – for far longer and more ardently than the first time. It didn't seem possible, but it felt even better than I remembered. Our kiss on Friday had been a goodbye kiss to end our date. But this was a kiss that didn't have to end, a kiss full of expectation, of the promise of things to come. There was no awkwardness, no first-time nerves or fear of clashing teeth. We just fitted together, mouth on mouth. While we kissed, Danny stroked my neck and the small of my back, sending tingles down my spine. I had my hands up the sleeves of his jacket, caressing his strong arms and shoulders through his T-shirt.

Nothing mattered when I kissed Danny – not the fact that I was still damp and cold, or that the hard, wooden bench was bruising my bottom, or even that, from time to time, other people walked past us and stared. (In fact, I rather liked that. I felt proud to be seen with such a gorgeous guy.) When I closed my eyes and kissed him I was as warm and as comfortable as I could ever hope to be. We were alone together in our own little bubble.

Occasionally, we would break off to hold each other silently and gaze into each other's eyes, as if we were trying to see far beyond the iris and the pupil to somewhere deeper, to a place that was secret and hidden. Once, Danny said, 'You have the most beautiful eyes, Naomi. I've never seen eyes that green before.' And I, never very good at accepting a compliment, had to ruin the moment by looking away.

By the time it started to grow dark, shortly after five, the rain had virtually stopped. With his arms still wrapped around me, Danny said, 'Why don't you come back to my house? It's a lot warmer and drier there and I make a mean hot chocolate.'

'That sounds divine,' I said, looking up at him. I was still damp and my mouth was dry and sore from kissing. 'Is it far? You've never actually told me where you live.'

'No,' he said. 'It's just the other side of the park, and then a bit. And I've brought the car.'

I was expecting Danny to drive a beaten-up old Ford or, perhaps, a Mini. But the only car in the car park was a red two-door, convertible sports car. I know barely anything about cars, but even I could tell it was expensive and very flash.

'I apologise for the car,' said Danny, in advance of any comment. 'My dad got me this when I passed my driving test. I think it was some sort of tax dodge for him. I loathe it – it's pretentious and brash and totally not me. I'd rather take the bus than drive this. I only brought it today because that picnic basket – which I *will* go back for later – is so bloody heavy.'

First Yellow, then the swanky restaurant, and now this car? And yet Danny said it was pretentious and brash. But he still drove it? I was confused. Was he worried that his wealth would put me off him? But then why had he taken me to those places? He was nothing if not contradictory. But, then again, I liked his air of mystery, the challenge of putting the pieces of the puzzle together.

He held open the car door for me and I climbed in. I'd

never been in a fast, expensive car before and just sitting there made me feel special, older and more sophisticated. I imagined myself arriving at a film premiere, flash bulbs popping from every angle. But, after what he'd just said, it didn't seem prudent to share my fantasy with Danny. Instead, I said, 'Yes, it's a bit over the top. I can see why you don't like it.'

If the car had surprised me, Danny's house was an even bigger shock. I knew his dad was a successful businessman and therefore, by implication, wealthy, but I had still imagined that his house would look like mine: a three-bedroom, semi-detached, with a front and back garden and a small garage. Pretty much everyone I knew lived in houses like that – suburban town houses built for mums and dads and their two-point-four kids. The hedges, doors and windows may have differed slightly, but the homes of all my family and friends were variations on a theme.

Danny's house was built to a different tune altogether. It was on one of the most exclusive streets in the area, where the residents hired private security guards and put up electric fences and surveillance cameras. It was set back from the street, at the end of a drive with electronic gates, which opened when Danny's car approached. I tried not to gasp when his house came into view. It was huge – at least four times the size of mine – and three storeys high, with a garden almost as big as the park. There were at least four cars parked outside, one of them just like Danny's, but in electric blue.

'Don't say anything,' said Danny sharply. 'I know what you must be thinking – that I'm some spoiled little rich kid who doesn't know he was born. I don't like living here; I'd rather be in a bedsit any day. It's just convenient, till I make The Wonderfulls a success. I don't want anything else to do with my parents or their filthy money!'

It was the first time I'd seen Danny so defensive. 'It's OK,' I said nervously. 'I'm not going to judge you. I like you for you. I don't care about where you live or what car you drive. Honestly.'

That seemed to reassure him. He squeezed my hand and smiled. 'All right, Naomi,' he said, in a calmer, gentler voice. 'Come in and get warm and I'll make you a hot chocolate.'

Danny had his own kitchen, in his own 'granny flat' at the side of his parents' house. It was entirely separate from the rest of the house, except it didn't have its own front door – you had to go through the main hall to get to it.

While he made the chocolate, he sent me off to look around his flat. He also had his own living room, bathroom, study (which he used as a storage room for his guitars) and a very messy bedroom (he must have forgotten he'd neglected to tidy it). His studio, which I didn't see that day, was in the basement, accessed by a flight of stairs from the kitchen. I gave each room a cursory glance; I didn't enjoy looking around on my own because it felt intrusive.

'How long have you lived in here?' I asked, coming back into the kitchen.

'Since I was sixteen,' he said, without looking up. He was stirring vigorously. 'My parents got sick of my noise and having my friends traipsing through their house and getting mud on their cream carpets. So they set me up in here and left me to my own devices.'

'You're lucky,' I said. 'I don't have any privacy.'

He shrugged. 'Maybe.'

We sat close together on Danny's leather sofa and sipped our hot chocolate in blissful silence. It was delicious – nothing like the powdered stuff I had at home, but thick and creamy, like warm, liquid chocolate mousse. I dreaded to think how many calories it contained. When Danny had cleared our cups away he asked if I minded if he played his guitar. 'I want to play you a few songs,' he said. I told him I'd love to hear them.

For the next couple of hours, he serenaded me, playing a mixture of his own compositions and some covers – Bowie, Nirvana, Oasis and Coldplay. It was good to hear stark, acoustic versions of The Wonderfulls' songs, without the frenzied guitars and heavy drums. Some of them were actually quite beautiful and tugged at my emotions with their aching melodies in minor keys. Where I could, I joined in, singing the harmony parts. Danny said he was impressed, that I had a sweet voice.

'We should get you in the band, doing backing vocals,' he said. I wasn't sure how seriously to take him, so I just blushed and smiled. The idea of standing up on stage and singing horrified me. The last time I'd tried – in a school concert five years before – I'd had such terrible stage fright that I'd dried up entirely, standing fixed to the stage in silent terror until one of the teachers rescued me.

When Danny's fingers grew tired of playing, he put

down his guitar and went into the kitchen to make us toasted cheese sandwiches. After we'd eaten and wiped the globules of melted cheese from our chins, he dimmed the lights, lit some candles and put on a chill-out CD. Then he spread himself out on the sofa and motioned that I should join him. I snuggled into his body, resting my head on his chest and hooking my legs around his so that I didn't fall off the edge. He stroked my hair and my face, placing his other arm around my waist. Self-consciously, I held in my tummy for as long as I could. For a while we just lay there, listening to each other's breathing, our eyes closed. From time to time he would pull me up towards him, so that I was almost lying on top of him, and we would kiss.

It's almost impossible to describe how good I felt. 'Nice' or 'warm' or 'lovely' or 'wonderful' or 'content' just don't sum it up. When you're a child and you have a tummy-ache and someone asks you what type of pain it is, you can't say, because you don't have the words to explain it – so you just say 'it hurts'. It was the same with the pleasure I felt while I was with Danny. I simply don't have the words in my vocabulary to explain it. All I knew was that I really couldn't be happier, physically or emotionally.

We must both have fallen asleep because when I next opened my eyes the candles had burned themselves out and the CD had finished playing. Trying not to wake Danny, I sat up and looked at my watch. It was eleven o'clock. I tip-toed into the bathroom and splashed some water on my face. My hair was dishevelled, my lips slightly swollen, and the skin around them red from kissing.

I heard Danny coming into the bathroom behind me. 'Hello, Omi,' he said, smiling. He yawned and stretched, rubbing his eyes with his hand. The side of his face was imprinted with creases and lines from the sofa. 'Are you OK?'

'Yes,' I said. 'Apart from a bit of stubble rash.'

He grinned. 'Occupational hazard.'

'Have you seen the time?' I asked. 'My parents will be worrying about me.'

He looked down at his watch. 'It's too late to go home now,' he said. 'Why don't you stay on the sofa? Call home while I go and get you a duvet and pillow.'

I hesitated before pulling my mobile phone out of my bag. Was 'sleep on the sofa' a euphemism for something I wasn't ready for? No, Danny deserved the benefit of the doubt. He had given me no reason not to trust him; he was so gentle and thoughtful.

I decided against calling my parents – I knew they would already be in bed. So, I texted Emily instead. HI EM. IT'S L8 SO STAYING WITH D'S PARENTS. TL M+D NT 2 WORRY. C U 2MORROW. NX

I knew she'd received it because a few moments later my mobile beeped and there was a message in return. It read: OK B GOOD X

'Everything all right?' asked Danny. I hadn't noticed him come back in. I nodded, a little shyly. He was carrying a double duvet and two pillows, which he must have taken from his own bed. He also had with him a huge, white T-shirt. 'For you to sleep in,' he said, handing it to me.

I went into the bathroom to change and squeezed out some of Danny's toothpaste, which I swished around my mouth with my finger. Once again, I conceded that I wouldn't be able to remove my make-up. *Danny really isn't good for my skin*, I thought. *But who cares?* I would gladly have endured a faceful of zits if it meant that I could spend the whole night just a few feet from Danny. *Just a few feet . . .* The realisation made me feel uneasy and excited at the same time. Did he intend to stay in his room all night, or would he tiptoe in to join me in the early hours? *No*, I decided again, *from all the evidence I've seen today I'm certain that Danny really is the perfect gentleman.*

When I came back into the living room I saw that he had already made up the sofa. He pulled the duvet aside and waited for me to climb in, before smoothing the cover over me. Nobody had tucked me in like that since I was a little girl.

'Goodnight, Omi,' he said, leaning over to give me one last, lingering kiss. He paused, as if he couldn't make up his mind about something, and then stroked my cheek. 'I'll see you in the morning,' he whispered. 'Sweet dreams.'

'Good night,' I said, smiling up at him. I felt happy and warm and protected. Looking back, I think it was at exactly *that* moment that I started truly loving Danny.

Chapter 7

I came round to the sound of a distant vacuum cleaner. Danny was standing over me, holding a cup of tea. He was wearing just a T-shirt and boxer shorts and I couldn't help noticing how unexpectedly good his legs were – strong and toned, like a footballer's.

'Good morning,' he whispered. 'That's just the cleaning lady in the main house. Don't worry, she doesn't come in here on Mondays.'

'What time is it?' I croaked.

'About ten,' said Danny. 'Pretty early for me, actually.'

'Ten? Oh my God!' I sat up, forgetting for an instant how dreadful I must look and then wishing I could hide back under the duvet. 'It's Monday. I was supposed to be at work an hour ago!'

'Oh.' Danny sounded disappointed. 'I suppose I could drive you there if you want.'

'But I haven't got my work clothes with me.' Now I was panicking.

'Calm down, Omi. It's not the end of the world. Look, why don't you call in sick and we can spend the day together.'

'No, I can't. I mean I shouldn't. Oh, I don't know!'

'What are they going to do to you? Arrest you?' he

gently mocked. 'Hang you? I don't think so. Go on, live dangerously.'

I thought about it for a second and then realised Danny was right. Calling in sick was simpler than going home, getting changed and then being two hours late. How would I explain that? And what could they do to me, anyway? I hadn't taken any time off sick before, not even when I genuinely didn't feel well. Surely one day was acceptable. They probably wouldn't even miss me.

'OK, I'll do it,' I said, before I could change my mind again. 'Danny Evans, you are a bad influence.'

I insisted that Danny leave the room and sent him off to get dressed while I made the call. I was worried I'd burst out laughing if I saw his face. I'd previously told him that my boss, Mr Stevens, was a stickler for discipline and Danny had done a wicked impression, marching around the room like a sergeant major, shouting 'Attention!'.

As I'd anticipated, the phone was answered by Kathy, the office receptionist.

'Hello, Kathy,' I said, in the huskiest voice I could muster. 'I'm really sorry, but,' (cough) 'I'm not very well today.'

'Oh, you poor love,' said Kathy, with so much sympathy that I felt guilty. 'You sound terrible. Don't you worry, I'll tell Mr Stevens. Now go back to bed and we'll see you when you're better.'

'Thanks,' I whispered, adding another cough for effect. 'I'm sure I'll be much better tomorrow.'

I hung up, sighing deeply. Danny had been waiting just

outside the door and he now came back in, grinning broadly. 'See, it wasn't so bad,' he said. 'Now drink your tea and then we'll decide what to do with the day.'

Content, he sat down next to me, leaning back against the cushions and crossing his legs. It was the first time I had seen him close up and jacketless, in sunlight. He was wearing a clean grey T-shirt and faded black jeans, which still smelled of washing powder. His forearms were lean and muscular, with a light covering of dark hair, and I could see his veins protruding. And then, when he stretched out his left arm towards me – I think he was intending to take my hand – I saw something else: a long, spidery pinkish mark, like an old scar. Next to it, there were other marks, some redder, some whiter, etching up and down his arm like doodles in a sketchbook.

'What's that?' I asked.

'What?' he exclaimed, surprised, snatching back his arm as if from a fire.

'That,' I said, pointing to the big scar. 'Did you hurt yourself? Was there an accident?'

He furrowed his brow. 'Yes,' he said. 'That's right, I had an accident, at school, a long time ago. It was nothing.' He appeared to shrink back from me, pulling himself up straight and staring into the distance. The action told me: *I don't want to talk about this now.*

'Poor Danny,' I said. My instincts told me there was more to it, but I didn't want to spoil what promised to be a perfect day. 'Poor Danny.' I didn't know what else to say, so I left it at that.

* * *

We spent a wonderful day together. I said I'd prefer not to go out anywhere, in case I bumped into someone from work, so we stayed in, listening to music and chatting about our pasts and our friends. We were filling each other in on the background to our lives, swapping anecdotes and memories. That's the funny thing about new relationships – you feel closer to your lover than to anyone else and yet you know virtually nothing about them, or they you. I didn't know what Danny's favourite colour was (he said green, like my eyes, but I think he was trying to flatter me), or whether he could dance or swim (he claimed he could do both, and well). He didn't know that I had broken my leg on a school trip to France five years earlier, or that I had a pet rabbit that had died, leaving me heartbroken when I was seven. I found out that Danny had appeared in a TV advert for a breakfast cereal when he was four; he was too embarrassed to show me the video clip and made me promise never to mention it again.

Telling each other these things is very important – you never know when the knowledge might come in handy.

'I'll remember never to order rabbit, then, when we go out to eat,' said Danny, with a dark grin.

'And I won't mention porridge. Ever,' I said, giggling.

I told Danny about Debbie and Holly and Natasha, and how much I missed them. I said I was certain he'd like them too and that he must meet them when they came home. He agreed, but, looking back, he didn't seem all that interested. He didn't ask many questions about my friends – not like I did when we discussed his – he just nodded and 'uh-huhed' in all the right places. I put it down to his being a 'bloke', but, if I'm honest, I was feeling a little hurt. My friends were important to me; I wanted them to be important to Danny too.

At the start of the day I'd made Danny promise that he would drop me home by four in the afternoon, so I could shower and change before Mum got back. I'd already decided I would pretend I had been to work and had simply left early. So, at three-fifteen, while Danny was showing me around his studio, trying (and failing) to impress me by twiddling various knobs and pressing odd buttons, I said, 'Danny, I think I'd better go home now.'

'Oh, Omi,' he said. 'Stay a bit longer. Can't you?'

'No.' I was insistent. If Dad found out I had skipped work I would never hear the end of it. I didn't want to tell Danny my reasons – he might have thought me childish.

'Go on,' teased Danny, tickling me under my chin. 'Just a few minutes.'

I giggled and squirmed. 'No, please, Danny. Now. Anyway, you've got to go and pick up the picnic basket from the park. If it's still there, which I doubt.'

'OK,' he said, with the exaggerated pout of a petulant little boy. 'I'll go and get my jacket and keys and your stuff. Wait for me in the hall by the front door.'

Danny took ages. I paced up and down the hall, stopping to admire the paintings on the wall (all originals) and the vases and other ornaments displayed on the sideboard. In my house we had vases from IKEA and Habitat, but the ones in Danny's house looked like museum pieces. I was carefully turning one around, so I could admire the ornate decoration on its handle, when I thought I heard the front door creak open behind me.

'Hello,' said a woman, with a deep, throaty and rather posh voice. 'And who might you be?' I jumped and turned simultaneously, almost knocking over the vase. The woman was extremely tall and elegant, with blond, sculpted hair. She was wearing an expensive–looking navy trouser suit and her make-up was perfectly applied, from her brown, pencilled-in brows to her blood-red talons.

'I'm Naomi,' I said, only too conscious of my own dismal appearance. I was wearing yesterday's muddy combats and I'd finger-combed my hair and applied new make-up over the remnants of the old. 'Hello.'

I moved forward to shake her hand, but she ignored me. Then she looked at me with disgust, as if I were a creature who had just stepped out of a swamp.

'Naomi who?'

'Naomi Waterman.' As soon as I said it I realised she hadn't wanted my surname. 'Er, Danny's Naomi.'

'I see,' she said, smirking. 'Well, I'm Danny's mother, Caroline Evans. I take it Danny is with you, or have you just wandered into my house on your own?'

Now I was upset. Why was this woman being so horrible to me? My mother would never have treated my friends or a boyfriend like this. She wouldn't have treated *anyone* like this.

'Of course not. Danny's gone to get his jacket so he can take me home. Sorry, I guess you didn't know I was here.'

She smirked again. 'Danny doesn't tend to talk to me about his girlfriends.' Perhaps I was being oversensitive, but I was sure she emphasised the 's'. 'Or,' she continued, 'very much at all, these days. I think it's easier for both of us that way.'

She walked towards me, and, for a second, I thought she was going to touch me, but then it became apparent that she was making for the stairs. 'Goodbye, Naomi,' she said as she went past. 'I trust you enjoyed your visit to my home.'

I must have looked shell-shocked, because when Danny appeared a minute or so later, the first thing he said was, 'What's the matter, Naomi? Are you OK?'

'Yes,' I said. 'I just met your mother.'

He nodded. 'That explains it. Did she give you a hard time?'

'Not really, but she wasn't very friendly.'

'Like I told you,' Danny spat. 'She's a cold bitch.'

The rage behind his words was chilling; I had never felt hate like that, and certainly not for my mother. I thought, *She must really have hurt him. What on earth did she do?* I was suddenly aware how little I knew about Danny's past, that he had lived twenty whole years before he met me. It made me feel uneasy.

I laughed nervously. 'I'm sure she's not that bad. Come on, Danny, please take me home now.'

'Sure,' he said, opening the front door. He put his arm around me and kissed me on the top of my head. I saw that he was smiling, but only with his mouth. His eyes were focused somewhere else, somewhere dark and desolate.

Chapter 8

The next few months were blissful. Danny and I spent as much time together as we could. He would pick me up from work and take me out for meals (I started to insist on paying half, even though it meant dipping into my university savings), or we'd go to the cinema or to a bar. At weekends we'd go to markets or galleries or tiny festivals in venues I didn't know existed, to hear performers that he'd read about in some obscure magazine. He opened my eyes to the city I'd lived in all my life, pointing out curiosities I wouldn't have noticed alone – a piece of ancient Roman wall on a modern street or a bizarre wig shop run by a couple in their eighties. When I was with Danny I saw the world in technicolour; it was like putting on a pair of 3-D glasses.

Sometimes we'd just stay in at his flat, have a takeaway and talk until the early hours. Whenever we were apart we were constantly on the phone, chatting and texting at every opportunity. I'd wake up to a HELLO message (usually sent in the small hours) and go to sleep reading, SWEET DREAMS, OMI.

Every minute that I spent with Danny made me fall in love with him a little more. I loved his spontaneity. I loved the way he turned up his nose and pouted when he was confused or deep in thought. I loved his funny little habits – the way he drank his tea, always taking a sip when it was still too hot and then appearing genuinely surprised when, once again, it burned his lips. I loved knowing that he kept all my texts, refusing to delete even the most mundane one until his message box was full. I loved the fact that he didn't appear to notice my flaws; he'd tell me how beautiful I looked without make-up and that he thought my body was perfect. He even laughed at my feeble jokes and when I mixed up my words; to him they were idiosyncracies, not idiocies.

There were thoughtful gestures, too. When, for example, I mentioned how much I enjoyed photography, he dug out an old Brownie box camera from his parents' attic and asked me to show him how to use it. Weeks after a silly conversation about sweets, during which I'd told him how I liked yellow ones best, he presented me with a jam-jar full of miscellaneous yellow sweets: wine gums, fruit gums and fruit pastilles, jellies and boiled sweets. He said he'd collected them from every packet he'd eaten and joked about the huge price he'd soon have to pay in dental bills. I later discovered that he had, in fact, been to his local supermarket, bought sackfuls of every tube and packet available, and carefully removed all the yellow sweets one by one, before discarding the rest.

He'd sit through *Friends* with me, even if it was an episode he'd seen at least three times before. He would come with me to watch tacky, romantic films because I had nobody else to see them with and, afterwards, he'd try to think of something good to say about the plot or the actors.

He'd cut stories out of newspapers if he thought I'd find them interesting and he'd scout eBay for vintage clothes I might like to check out. When I had a cold he tucked me up on his sofa and brought me gallons of freshly squeezed orange juice and made me tomato soup and boiled eggs with soldiers because I'd told him that was my favourite comfort food.

I could go on and on. I could probably fill a whole book with lists of what I liked about Danny. But no amount of examples would sum up why I felt so strongly about him. What makes you love someone has little to do with the number of wonderful qualities they possess. It's about glimpsing something inside them that nobody else can see and realising you've always needed it, even though you didn't know you were looking. It's about inventing a reality that is true only for the two of you.

Meeting Danny on the bus no longer seemed like mere accident. It was fated: I had been meant to catch that particular bus because Danny would get on it. This belief was sealed when Danny told me that he'd seen another bus coming first, but had made a split-second decision not to run for it. It didn't occur to me that he might have felt too tired or too lazy to run; it was simply meant to be. I credited other coincidences with the same, irrational significance: the fact that we had matching birthmarks on our collarbones, for example, gave us a unique bond. I ignored the probability that thousands of other people probably had a birthmark in the same place.

Whenever I thought about Danny my heart beat faster

and it brought a strange sensation – half pleasure, half nausea – to the pit of my stomach. It made me smile to myself and flush all over. I knew that what I felt for Danny must be love – at least, this was how I'd always imagined love to be – but somehow I could never say it. Even though the things he said and did made me fairly certain he felt the same way, there was a tiny part of me that was afraid he might not say 'I love you' back. What if he were to laugh? Or say, 'Sorry, Naomi, I like you a lot, but I don't feel like that about you.' I didn't want to risk breaking the spell. Sometimes, we'd look at each other for long, silent minutes, and the words would be on the tip of my tongue, but I'd swallow them back down again. I needed to hear them from him first.

Christmas was an ordeal that year, because it meant four whole days away from Danny. He was spending it with friends and had invited me to join him, but I didn't even dare ask my parents. Missing our annual family celebration would be considered a crime almost on a par with mugging an old lady – so heinous that I might as well pack my bags and never return. So, as always, Dad drove us up to Nottingham to stay with my uncle's family. In the past I'd always looked forward to it. I'd enjoyed packing the car with presents to be opened on Christmas morning and I liked spending time with my younger cousins. But that year, every mile on the motorway was another mile further from Danny. I didn't care what my parents had bought me (even though I got the funky speakers for my iPod that I'd wanted for months), and I couldn't be bothered to help the little ones put batteries in their new toys. On Christmas Day, all I was interested in was having some time to myself, so I could open Danny's present.

I finally unwrapped it late in the afternoon, in the guest bedroom I shared with Emily, while the children were happily playing and my older relatives were dozing on the sofas. I was like a little girl all over again, fumbling at the shiny paper, desperate to see inside. Danny had bought me a gorgeous, sea-green cashmere sweater – the softest, most beautiful thing I'd ever seen, let alone owned. It was almost too nice to wear. For a while, I just hugged it, as if it were a teddy bear, thinking warm thoughts about Danny and giving myself butterflies.

Emily came into the room while I was trying it on. 'Wow!' she exclaimed enviously. 'It's lovely, Nay.' Then she peered at the label – from a posh, designer shop – and raised her eyebrows. 'How can he afford it?'

'I dunno,' I said. 'His gigs, maybe? Or his savings? I think he also got some money when his grandad died.' But the same thought had crossed my mind. I'd pushed it away, as I always did then. I had no time for such thoughts, for questions without resolution.

'What did you get him?'

'Some CDs and a really nice, leather-bound book for him to write his songs in.'

'Oh,' she said.

'I know.' I'd spent hours choosing Danny's presents, but now they seemed inadequate.

'God, Nay, he must really like you.'

'Do you think?' I asked, smiling. 'I really miss him. I know it's only for a few days, but it feels like forever.'

'Wow,' she said. 'You're really smitten.'

'I think he's the one, Em. He totally gets me, you know? I think he's my soulmate.'

Emily was embarrassed. We'd talked about Danny before, of course, but I hadn't gone this far with her. She wasn't a romantic like me and she preferred to keep her feelings hidden. 'I've never seen you like this,' she said, for once, apparently at a loss for words. 'I'll leave you alone, so you can call him.'

It was the first time I had articulated my feelings about Danny. Ever since I was little and had read about princes and princesses in fairy tales, I'd believed that there was someone out there who would complete me, my other half – my soulmate. It had never been clear what I was looking for – there were no criteria to cross off a list – but I was as certain as I could be that I had found him in Danny. I had only my feelings to go on, but what else is there?

The tedium of work no longer bothered me. I was happy to stand alone in the photocopying room, whiling away the hours daydreaming of Danny. I stopped asking for more interesting tasks and now rarely volunteered to sit in on case meetings as a note-taker. Late nights at Danny's meant that I often slept in and consequently arrived at work later than I should, and I never worked a minute past five-thirty. If my boss disapproved, I didn't notice. I had lost all interest in the

legal practice; I may as well have been working in a supermarket or on a factory production line.

When all my sentences began to start and end with 'Danny',
my parents realised I must be serious about him and decided
it was now time to invite him for Sunday lunch. To my relief,
he arrived on time – which was a first – and he was dressed
smartly, in a blue cotton sweater and grey trousers. He
shook my parents' hands and called them 'Mr and Mrs
Waterman' until they insisted they'd prefer David and
Martha. He complimented my mother on her cooking and
my father on his choice of wine. He even indulged my father
by discussing share prices and the implications of the latest
European directive. Emily shot me questioning looks and
giggled behind her hand. After Danny had left, Dad said
what a nice, intelligent young man he was, and Mum
declared him 'charming'.

I must admit I found it all rather odd. The Danny I
knew and loved – the scruffy, affectionate joker – was
nowhere to be seen that day. He kissed me on the cheek
when he came in, but after that, he didn't touch me all afternoon, and I could only surmise it was for fear of offending
my parents. Even his voice was different, the lazy drawl
replaced by clearly pronounced, public-school English. It
was like dating Superman and then one day finding myself
with Clark Kent instead. I wondered which was the real
Danny and which the mask: this perfect gentleman or the
edgy rock-and-roll dreamer? Could he really be both
people, at the same time?

When I mentioned it on the phone later that evening, he didn't understand why I was perturbed.

'I was just being the person they wanted me to be,' he said, sounding a little annoyed. 'I'm the same guy and I feel exactly the same way about you as I always have. But I'm not exactly going to snog you in front of your parents, am I?'

'Of course not,' I said, frustrated. I was finding it hard to articulate my feelings, or to figure out why I was so bothered. How could I tell him that I feared I didn't know or understand him as well as I'd believed? How, when I didn't even want to admit it to myself? 'It's not that. I just wanted them to see what I see.'

'Look, they liked me and that's what you wanted. Or would you have preferred it if I'd come in half-loaded and ignored them?'

'No. It's just . . . Oh, it doesn't matter.'

I dropped the conversation. Perhaps I should have tried harder, but I didn't want to make a fuss. Somewhere, at the back of my mind, a subconscious feeling was beginning to form: the worry that if I pushed Danny too hard I might push him away. And it was easy enough to convince myself that he was right. Life would be so much simpler if my parents liked him. I decided I could learn to live with the clean-cut version of Danny, so long as he only appeared every couple of Sundays at my parents' house.

As Danny had promised, I became a regular at The Wonderfulls' gigs. They played various pubs and venues around North London and always got good write-ups in the local press. The groupies no longer worried me. As soon as Danny came off stage we'd disappear out of the back door together, leaving his gaggle of girl fans waiting, disappointed, in the bar.

Danny asked if I would help with The Wonderfulls' website, which featured photos, lyrics, snatches of songs to download and upcoming gig dates. I enjoyed typing in reviews and adding new pictures. I'd always liked taking photos and I became the group's unofficial photographer, snapping away at gigs and making everyone pose for portraits and group shots backstage. I kept the best portrait of Danny for myself, framing it and putting it on my bedside table so I could see him as soon as I woke up. Unlike the other pictures, which showed Danny in rock-star guise, pouting and preening for the camera, I felt that this photo captured 'my' Danny. In it he was looking away to the side, his eyes focused on a distant point and his lips slightly parted, as if he was about to speak. He said he didn't like the photo, but he would never explain why.

I was also invited to rehearsals, which usually took place at Danny's flat on Tuesday and Wednesday evenings. The other band members seemed to like me – or at least tolerate me – and I grew fond of Mike, the keyboard player, who always took the trouble to find out how I was and what I'd been doing. I wasn't so sure about the others. The drummer, Pete, was withdrawn and hard to talk to; the bass guitarist, Dylan, was a pot-head who didn't seem capable of intelligent conversation; and Andy, the lead guitarist, had been at school with Danny, and just seemed arrogant. I didn't like the way he tried to alter Danny's songs, imprinting them with his own arrangements and ideas, not because it improved them, but just so that he could make his mark.

I was always careful not to get in the way or to give my opinion when it wasn't wanted. Often, I'd make my excuses and go and sit in Danny's bedroom to watch TV or read. But Danny said he liked having me there; he called me his muse. The word filled me with pride. I had always looked at paintings in galleries and wondered about the artists' muses, their faces captured for all eternity. I didn't have the talent or the confidence then to create anything valuable myself, so being somebody else's inspiration seemed to me almost as great an accomplishment as being the artist.

From what I could see, The Wonderfulls didn't get much playing done at rehearsals. They'd sit around smoking and drinking, talking about other bands and football. I knew it wasn't my place to say anything, but I couldn't understand why I was the only person who seemed concerned. In a couple of weeks, they would be watched by an A & R guy, who had it in his power to give them a record contract. They might not have another chance. But what did I know?

Chapter 9

Late one Wednesday night, when I'd arrived home from rehearsals at Danny's and I was getting ready to go to bed, my mobile rang. I knew it couldn't be Danny because it wasn't his ring (a tinny version of a Nirvana track which I'd downloaded from the Internet), and I thought about letting it go straight to my message box. The number didn't look familiar and I couldn't imagine who might be calling me so late. But although I didn't really feel like talking to anyone, curiosity got the better of me and I picked up.

It was Debbie. We'd spoken several times over the Christmas holidays, but she'd gone away with her family and we hadn't managed to see each other. Since she'd returned to university we'd fallen back into a pattern of irregular communication.

'Hi, Naomi,' she said. Her voice was quiet and she sounded anxious.

'Deb?' I said. 'Are you OK? I didn't recognise your number.'

'I'm using Sam's phone,' she said. I could tell she was on the brink of tears. 'I got mugged.'

'Oh no, that's awful! Are you OK?'

'Yes, I guess. I was just going into a club and I saw this guy coming towards me and he grabbed my bag and shoved me really hard. It all happened so fast I couldn't even scream.'

'Are you OK?' I asked again. We'd hardly spoken in weeks and even though I felt sorry for her I was very aware of the distance between us. I wanted to hug her, but she was in a different city so I couldn't. I couldn't even picture where she was or whom she was with, and I didn't know what to say to make her feel better.

'My bag had all my stuff in it – my mobile, keys, ID, all my cash . . .'

'What a nightmare. Have you told the police?'

'Yes, and I've cancelled my cards. I don't know, I guess I just wanted to hear a friendly voice. You don't mind me calling, do you?'

'Of course not,' I said, emphatically. I was pleased it was me she'd chosen to call.

'I think I'm going to come home at the weekend. I'm feeling a bit homesick. It would be really nice to see you.'

'Yes,' I said, recalling the plans I'd made with Danny for the weekend. He didn't have a gig and we were supposed to be driving down to Brighton to meet some friends of his. But I couldn't let Debbie down – and I did want to see her. Brighton would keep. 'Yes, it would be nice to see you too.'

'Maybe I could stay over on Saturday?' she asked tentatively. 'It would be like old times. We could get a DVD or something.'

'Sure,' I said. 'That would be lovely.'

'That's great,' she said, sounding more cheerful. 'I'm

looking forward to it. I'll give you a call when I get home on Friday.'

After we'd said our goodbyes I went to my wardrobe and took out my old photograph albums, which I stored on the top shelf behind my jumpers. I wanted to remind myself of the good times I'd shared with Debbie – the joint birthday parties and sleepovers and holidays abroad with her parents or mine. I couldn't remember a time when I hadn't known her. We'd met on the first day of primary school and had become firm friends at once, hugging each other and declaring proudly that we were 'best friends', in the possessive way that little girls do. Other friends had come and gone, groups had formed and splintered, but Debbie and I had remained solid, protecting one another from the bitching and the name-calling. She was the first person I told when I'd started my period; she'd bought me my first lip-gloss; we'd both enjoyed our first snogs during a game of spin the bottle at her thirteenth birthday party.

And here, in the tattered albums, was the documentary evidence of our friendship. There we were, at seven, standing in a playground somewhere, our arms wrapped around each other, grinning broadly. And there at fourteen, in crop tops and hipster jeans (which did nothing for either of us), with badly applied make-up and terrible hair. Here I was, last year, sitting on a beach in Greece in a bikini, my arms folded protectively over my belly, while Debbie stood next to me in a T-shirt because she'd sunburned her shoulders the day before.

Thumbing through the pages made me grin and cringe in

equal measures, as I witnessed my transformation from a sweet-looking, freckle-faced child to an awkward and self-conscious teenager. It was like viewing one of those computer programmes the police use to show what a toddler who'd disappeared ten years before might look like now. My face had visibly thinned and lengthened over the years, while my nose and chin had become more prominent. My hair, which had been through a remarkable range of styles, had darkened and curled, and my body had filled out. Debbie had changed too. She had always been thin and flat-chested, but in the past few years she'd become less of a tomboy, growing her hair and wearing skirts, and replacing her glasses with contact lenses. She said I was the pretty one, but I could never see it. I envied her long legs and flat tummy, the fact that her hair didn't frizz in the rain and that she never got zits. I wondered if she'd look different after a few of months away at university. It made me sad to think that now she would have new photographs in which I didn't feature, her arms around people I didn't recognise.

It niggled me that Debbie was only coming home because she'd been mugged. But maybe having something horrible happen to her had made her realise how much she missed me, that her real friends were the people she'd known for years. Maybe things would be just like they used to be. I looked forward to spending time with her, to staying up into the early hours and chatting until one of us fell asleep. Best of all, Danny would finally meet her and the three of us could hang out together, like a perfect triangle made up of the most important people in my life.

For the first time in months I went to sleep thinking not of Danny, but of Debbie. I dreamed that we were at her house, playing hide-and-seek. We'd locked ourselves into her bedroom and were cowering together behind her bed. Somebody – a faceless man with dark hair – was banging on the door, trying to get in. As he forced his way into the room, I woke up.

The following evening Danny and I went out for a curry. I kept meaning to tell him Debbie was coming home at the weekend, but the time never seemed right. He was in a particularly sweet and silly mood and I didn't want to spoil it. What do you do, interrupt a funny story to say, 'That's hysterical, Danny, and by the way, I can't go to Brighton'? Of course I knew even then that it was just an excuse. The truth was, I knew he'd be angry and I didn't want a fight. I've never been very good at arguing – I end up getting upset, then crying, which usually makes the other person feel even more frustrated.

So, it wasn't until later, when we were sitting in his car outside my house that I mentioned it.

'You know we were going to go to Brighton on Saturday?' I asked nervously. 'Well, would it be OK if we did it another weekend?'

'Why?' he said, smirking. 'You aren't shy about meeting my mates, are you?'

'No,' I said, laughing, although there was some truth in it. 'Actually, it's because of one of *my* mates. You know my best friend, Debbie? Well, she's coming home for the weekend.'

'I see,' he said, clearly irritated. 'And you want to see her instead?'

'No, not instead. I want you to come out with us too. But I do really want to spend some time with her.'

'But Brighton's all arranged. Can't you see her another weekend?'

'No, she's upset. She had her bag nicked. Look, I couldn't really say no.'

'You never can,' he muttered.

The comment was like a knife in my belly. Was that how he really saw me – weak and pliable? Or was he just trying to goad me?

'What's that supposed to mean?'

'Nothing.' He wasn't looking at me. 'Just that you've done nothing but bitch about her ever since you've known me and now you want to drop everything for her when she snaps her fingers. I thought you were stronger than that.'

'It's not like that, Danny,' I said, my voice beginning to break. I could feel tears welling up in my eyes. Danny and I had never before exchanged a cross word, but now I was receiving the icy treatment I had feared. He wouldn't even touch me. When I tried to put my hand on his arm he flinched and brushed it away. 'I was pissed off with her because she didn't seem to care as much as she used to. I was scared I was losing her. Now, she wants to come home and maybe if we spend some time together things will be how they were.'

'No, she wants to come home because she's a silly girl who didn't keep her eye on her bag and feels homesick.'

Hearing Danny echo my own niggling doubts made me feel defensive. 'That's not fair. You don't even know her. She's lovely. You'll see.'

'I'm not sure I can be arsed,' he stated harshly.

'What do you mean?' It was so important to me that Danny and Debbie got on. I was trying hard to stay cool, not to let myself cry. I felt shocked and angry and self-protective at the same time and I didn't know what to do with all those emotions.

'I mean I don't see the point of hanging round with you and your so-called best mate when I could be in Brighton having a great time.'

'Don't you want to meet my friends? I've met yours. I spend loads of time with the band.'

'That's different,' he snapped. 'And you know it. I do want to meet your friends, some time, but not when it means I have to cancel something we were both looking for-ward to.'

At last, he turned to look at me. Noticing that a fat tear was beginning to roll down my cheek, he softened. 'I'm sorry, Omi,' he said, wiping it away with his hand. 'I didn't mean to upset you.'

It wasn't enough. The worry that he wasn't really inter-ested in my friends had troubled me for many weeks. I made a point of turning my head away from him.

'But you have upset me,' I said. 'I'm sorry about Saturday, but Brighton's not about to fall into the sea – we can go another time. I just feel that you don't care about my friends. I know nobody's around at the moment and I must seem like Billy No-mates, but my friends are important to me and when they're here I want to see them. They're part of me. If you don't meet my friends, how can you really know me?'

Now *he* was upset. 'How can you say that? I know you better than anyone. I know everything about you and you know everything about me. I don't need to meet Debbie to know that.'

'But you do!' I cried. I opened the car door and put my left foot on the kerb. I didn't want him to see me sobbing and I could feel a gush of tears waiting to escape.

'You're being ridiculous,' he tutted, grabbing my arm in an attempt to stop me from getting out the car. 'You know what? Let's forget this weekend. You do whatever you want to do with Debbie and I'll go to Brighton.'

'Fine,' I barked, shaking him off me. 'Whatever.' I launched myself out of my seat and slammed the car door behind me. For a moment I thought he might follow me, but then I heard the roar of the engine and the squeal of tyres as he sped away up the street. Tears streaming down my face, I let myself into my house and, exhausted, went straight to bed. I cried myself to sleep.

So there it was: our first argument. My grandma once told me that nothing lasts, and nothing – good or bad – stays the same. I didn't really understand what she meant until that night. I'd genuinely believed that we would remain in our happy state forever. I saw us always laughing, always agreeing, always on the same page. It's naïve, I know, but I had never truly allowed myself to accept that Danny could be cruel to me – I'd hoped his feelings for me some-how granted me immunity. The argument brought me back to reality and, worse, it made me feel alone again.

There was no text from Danny when I awoke the next morning. I made myself go into work and do what needed to be done. I tried to spend as much time as I could with the other staff members, so I didn't have time to think about Danny. Whenever there was silence our argument began to replay over and over in my mind, like my dad's old vinyl records when they got stuck. But I couldn't ignore the nauseous feeling in the pit of my stomach that wouldn't go away. Surely this wasn't the end? It couldn't be. The thought of losing Danny terrified me and yet I couldn't bring myself to contact him first. All day, I toyed with the idea of calling or texting him, but what would I say? Sorry? I hadn't done anything wrong, so why should I apologise? Perhaps I should send him a jokey text pretending that nothing had happened. But that would just be letting him get away with it.

At three in the afternoon, Danny put me out of my misery by texting me. DECIDED 2 GO TO BTN 2DAY. HV GD TIME WIV D. DX. I read and reread the text countless times, trying to decide what it meant. There was no apology, no mention of the argument and he had stuck to his guns and gone to Brighton – and a day early too. Nothing had been resolved. Then again, he had wished me well and finished with a kiss – surely that was a positive sign?

It took me over an hour to reply. After deleting at least

ten possible messages, I settled on the concise: OK. SPK WHEN
UR BACK. NX. Its brevity, in contrast to my usual messages –
and the fact that I'd signed my name with an 'N', not an
'O' – showed I was still unhappy and hadn't entirely forgiven him, but it wasn't nasty and it left things open.

Emily agreed that I'd got the tone right. 'You don't
want to let him think he's got away with it,' she said, angry
on my behalf. It was lovely that she felt so protective of me.
She'd made me run through the argument several times,
punctuating the end of Danny's words with the occasional
'bastard' and 'selfish git' until she realised her vehemence
was making me more upset.

'He'll come running back,' she said. 'Anyone can see
how much he likes you. Just make him sweat a bit first.'

I wondered where she'd learned so much about guys.
Wasn't I the big sister here? Still, I allowed myself to be
reassured.

Now, I just had to get through the next two days.

Debbie came home that evening. She was spending Friday
night with her parents and we'd arranged to meet on
Saturday lunchtime at a coffee shop in town, and then do a
bit of window shopping and come back to my house to
watch a DVD. I was determined to have a good time with
Debbie, to prove to myself that I could still have fun without Danny and, more importantly, to reassure myself that
she was still my best friend.

I spent Friday night watching TV with my parents
(Emily was at a friend's house). Anything was better than

sitting alone in my bedroom, dwelling on what had happened. Mum and Dad seemed surprised that I wanted to be
with them and even more surprised that I appeared happy
to watch an hour-long documentary about medieval archi-
tecture. I was very quiet and Mum kept asking if I was all
right. I told her Danny was at a family do and that I fancied
an evening in because I was tired. I'm not sure she believed
me, but she knew better than to pry.

I felt far less anxious in the morning, after a good night's
dreamless sleep. I went into town early and wandered round
the shops on my own, testing lip-gloss and blushers. Debbie
was already drinking a cappuccino when I arrived at the café.
She was dressed more scruffily than I'd seen her in years, in
ripped jeans and a baggy jumper. Despite her concessions to
the 'student' look, she still looked smart and polished, her
hair a little too neat and glossy. It made me smile to myself.
She hadn't changed, really.

'Naomi!' she cried, when she saw me come in. She
bounded out of her chair and rushed over to kiss me hello.
I was happy and reassured that she seemed so genuinely
pleased to see me. I hugged her. When I put my arms
around her I could feel the bones in her back.

'You've lost so much weight!' I exclaimed. 'Don't they
feed you at university?'

'I know,' she said, embarrassed. 'It's terrible. That's
what a diet of Pot Noodles and toasted sandwiches does to
you. My mum was horrified. After Christmas she sent me
back with a month's supply of nutritious food.' She looked
me up and down. 'Hey, you look good, though.'

'Thanks.' I blushed. I was about to say, 'That's what being in love does for you', but given that Danny and I were barely on speaking terms, it didn't seem appropriate. Instead, I asked, 'So, do you want to hit the shops, then?'

'Great. I have absolutely no money and no plastic, so I won't be able to do any damage.'

'You can help me buy something,' I said, laughing.

We spent the afternoon trawling the rails of all the high street stores and chatting about everything under the sun. Although I was pleased that Debbie finally seemed interested in the details of my life, I wasn't in the mood for serious talk; every time she asked about me I deflected the conversation back to her. I had always been a good listener, so she didn't notice. She had so much news to tell me that a simple question, such as 'What's your accommodation like?' could elicit a ten-minute speech full of anecdotes involving copious amounts of alcohol and guys I'd never heard of.

To be honest, I was relieved that we were getting on so well. I felt comfortable in Debbie's company – it seemed almost as if she'd never been away. I decided to forgive her for her laxity in calling and her apparent disinterest in my life during our telephone conversations. It wasn't her fault, I told myself. She obviously didn't get much privacy in her hall of residence and it sounded like there was so much going on that she really didn't have any time. She'd simply stored thoughts of life back home in a little box at the back of her mind.

When our feet grew sore and our eyes bleary, we headed back to my house. Mum and Dad were delighted to see Debbie. They'd never told me directly, but I knew they thought she was a good influence. She was the sensible one, the one who'd always known what she wanted to do – to become a teacher – and hadn't wavered. She'd gone straight from school to university and, in four years' time, would come out with her teaching degree and, no doubt, step straight into a good job. She was intelligent and polite and reliable: the qualities my dad thought most important. Often, if I was rude or disagreed with him, he'd say, 'I bet Debbie doesn't talk like that to her father.' I found it irritating, especially as I knew Dad's opinion of Debbie was wrong. If she'd been as boring as he thought her, we would never have been friends. The Debbie I knew was fun, a bit of a bitch and a terrible flirt. She'd had far more boyfriends than me; guys liked her because not only did she have great legs, but she also loved football and could act like one of the lads.

My parents wanted us to join them for dinner, but we said we'd already agreed to get a Chinese takeaway – my treat. We escaped upstairs and ran into my bedroom, locking the door so that nobody could disturb us. Debbie perched on my bed, as she had done a thousand times before. 'Your room looks exactly the same,' she said. I wasn't sure if it was a criticism or a compliment.

'Course it does,' I replied. 'No point changing it now.'

'I guess not,' she said. 'It's weird sleeping in my bedroom at home. It doesn't feel like mine any more.' She glanced across me and her eyes came to rest on the photograph of Danny. 'Is that Danny, then?'

'Yes,' I said, with a mixture of pride and sadness. I looked at the picture and realised that I now knew every part of his face, every angle, almost as well as my own.

'Oh, he's not what I expected. He looks like a bit of a poser.'

Debbie had a tendency to be blunt – it often got her into trouble – but I hadn't expected her to be so unkind.

'What do you mean?' I asked, unable to conceal my defensiveness.

'Oh, you know, the designer stubble, the long hair and that faraway look in his eyes. He's not your normal type, is he?'

'And what's my normal type?'

'You know, like Mark or Jack – boyish, clean-cut, fair . . .'

'Actually, they *weren't* my type,' I snapped, irritated. 'They're more your type. I think Danny is gorgeous.'

'OK, sorry. Don't be so touchy. He is good-looking, just not what I imagined. So what's he doing tonight? I kind of thought – hoped – I might meet him.'

'He had to go to Brighton,' I said, trying desperately not to show that I was upset. 'I was supposed to go with him, but then you said you were coming home and I cancelled.'

'Oh Naomi, I'm sorry.' She sounded like she felt guilty.

I decided to tell her the whole story. 'Actually, we had an argument about it. It's pathetic, really, but we haven't spoken properly since. That's why I haven't said much about him today.'

'I didn't realise. You should have said.'

'It's OK. We can go to Brighton any time.'

'So why aren't you speaking?'

Now I wished I hadn't mentioned the argument. How could I tell her that Danny didn't want to meet her?

'You didn't give me much notice . . . and it all kind of got blown out of proportion.'

'Sorry,' she said, her tone sarcastic now. 'Next time I'm mugged I'll make sure Danny's informed well in advance.'

I laughed, but the damage was done. I'd wanted Debbie to be excited about Danny, to congratulate me on finding a wonderful, handsome, interesting guy. Instead, she appeared to dislike him already – and they hadn't even met.

Debbie took a deep breath. 'I'm sorry, Naomi,' she said. 'I'm your best mate. If I can't be honest with you, who can? I want you to be happy, and I know you really like Danny – you always seem so excited about him on the phone – but he sounds so intense and temperamental. I've known you forever and I've never seen you so moody and snappy. And he's got you caught up in his silly dream of being a pop star. Are you sure he's good for you?'

How could she say that? She must have had some idea how happy Danny made me, even if she hadn't seen us together. She didn't know how interesting our conversations were, how much he'd taught me about music and books and politics. Just *being* with Danny was a buzz.

'It's not a silly dream,' I said. 'He's talented and ambitious and creative . . .'

She interrupted me. 'Ambitious? You told me he dropped out of Oxford.'

'So? He left to follow his dream – that's pretty ambitious in my book. At least he was bright enough to get in.'

I knew my comment was cruel. Debbie had wanted to go to Oxford, but she hadn't achieved high enough grades in her A-levels. I had never worked as hard as her at school, but I always did better; it was something we never spoke about.

'Piss off,' she spat. 'That was below the belt. Anyway, I'm glad I didn't go to snobby Oxford now. I feel right at home at Manchester and from what I've heard, it's much more fun.'

We both sat silently for a few minutes, sulking. Yet another evening with somebody I cared about had turned into a bickering session. I appeared to have developed a talent for it.

'Sorry,' I said, eventually. 'I take it back. Look, let's call a truce. We'll go and get the takeaway and you can choose the film, OK?'

'OK,' she said. 'Nothing arty or French. I fancy a rom-com.'

'Deal.'

We made the best of the remainder of the night, eating too much and giggling at the movie, which was about a dumb, blonde American girl who gets herself into lots of scrapes, but – surprise, surprise – wins the gorgeous guy in the end. But my heart wasn't in it. I kept losing concentration and thinking about Danny and how much I loved being with him. I decided that when he arrived home I would call him and tell him I'd been stupid and that he was right about Debbie. My time with her had only confirmed what he'd said and what I'd feared: Debbie didn't really understand me any more. She didn't *get* me – not like he did.

At midnight, Debbie said, 'Do you mind if I call a cab? I know I was going to sleep over, but my parents want me to see my gran tomorrow and then I've got to get the train back.'

'Oh, Deb,' I said, aware that I was losing my last chance to make things right with her. 'It would have been fun,' I added, with little conviction, but it seemed the right thing to say.

'Yeah, but I'm knackered. I promise I'll come and see you again soon. And you've got to come up and stay with me too. We must arrange it.'

'Sure,' I said. 'That would be good.' We hugged each other, as we always had, but I felt no pleasure in it, no security or warmth. It was like hugging a distant relative at a funeral.

Emily arrived home a few minutes after Debbie had left. She came into my room and excitedly began to tell me about the party she'd been to and how the guy she'd really liked for ages had kissed her. I tried to feign interest, but then she noticed how sad I looked and stopped mid-sentence.

'Are you OK, Naomi? You seem so miserable. Where's Debbie? I thought she was staying.'

'She went home,' I said. 'I think we've grown apart.'

'But you've been, like, best mates for years.'

'Yes. I guess things change.'

She rubbed my arm affectionately. 'I'm sure you'll sort it out.'

'I don't think so. Maybe we were never as close as I thought and it took her going away to make me realise. And she doesn't like Danny.'

'What?' Emily cried. 'When did she meet him?'

'She hasn't. She didn't like his picture and she actually said she thought he was bad for me.'

'That's ridiculous! I think he's great, not to mention incredibly good-looking. I know you've had a bit of a barny and he was out of order and I called him a bastard, but I didn't mean it. You'll get it all sorted, I know you will.'

I really appreciated Emily's support. She may have been angry with Danny on my behalf the day before, but she genuinely cared about him. She had been out with us several times and Danny had been very sweet to her, letting her come backstage after a gig and introducing her to the band. She'd told me her school friends thought he was really cool which, by association, made her cool too. She'd even said that she looked forward to Sunday lunches now that he was a regular guest.

'I hope so,' I said.

'You're perfect for each other, Nay. Anyone can see that.'

'Thanks, Em,' I said. 'You've really made me feel better.'

And she had.

Chapter 10

Sunday was the longest day. I itched to call Danny, checking my mobile and my watch every few minutes, wondering if it was too soon to call, whether he would be home yet, if he would ring me. I ate lunch with my parents, went for a walk in the park, bought myself a glossy magazine and read it page by page. Still, I heard nothing. By five p.m., I was restless and sick with nerves, fussing with my hair and my clothes and chewing the skin around my fingernails. The words I had confidently planned – and rehearsed – to say to Danny no longer seemed appropriate. Like any words repeated too often, they had become meaningless, nonsensical, a jumble of syllables and sounds. *'Hi Danny,'* I had intended to say. *'I'm so glad you're back. Haven't we been a couple of idiots? I've missed you and can't wait to see you.'* But the longer I waited, the more my courage deserted me. I was afraid that if I dialled his number and he replied, all that would come out of my mouth was 'Dann*yyyyyyyyy . . .*'

The way things were, it would not have been sensible to send him another text. It's so hard to choose the right words, to make sure they don't have any other, unintended meanings. You can text something with one tone of voice in mind and it will be read in quite another. And, even at the best of times, Danny, always perceptive, had a tendency to analyse everything, to read between the lines. That day, even the inauspicious use of a question mark could have made things a hundred times worse.

Why hadn't he called? Surely he must be home by now. Had he met somebody else in Brighton? Had something happened – a fight, an accident? Was he lying in a hospital somewhere, alone and frightened, unable to call me? I knew I was letting my imagination run away with me, but the idea that he was injured seemed preferable to the alternative explanations: that he simply didn't want to talk to me, or worse, that he was over me.

At about seven in the evening, I put on my coat and told my parents I was going to the twenty-four-hour garage up the road to buy some cotton wool so I could paint my toenails. I couldn't think of any other reasonable-sounding excuse for going out on a cold and rainy Sunday evening. I figured that the walk would kill a good twenty minutes.

I was about to open the front door when I noticed a small, white envelope lying on the doormat. *That's odd*, I thought. *We don't get post on a Sunday*. It didn't look like a pizza-delivery flyer or a leaflet advertising window cleaning services. I bent down to pick it up and, on turning it over, saw that it was addressed to me. There was no stamp, just my name and address, handwritten. I recognised the writing immediately: it was Danny's. I had seen the same slanted, curly-topped lettering in the books of song lyrics he had let me read, and he had used the same purple ink.

Why had Danny written to me? When had he delivered this? He must have been here, at my house, while I sat in my bedroom upstairs. Why hadn't he rung the doorbell? I was breathing faster now, my heart beating loud and erratically against the wall of my chest. Still crouching in the hallway, my hands shaking, I ripped open the envelope. As I pulled out the three neatly folded sheets within, a five-pound note fluttered to the floor. I was confused. Why had Danny given me money? What did he have to say that he had to write down?

I don't have to try to remember the contents of the letter – I have kept it, to this day, with all my old photographs and mementoes, in a little trunk under my bed. Even now, it pains me to read it.

Dear Omi,

Please find enclosed the fiver you lent me the other night. I will give you back the books and CDs that I borrowed soon. It's two p.m. and I'm perfectly sober. Please bear with me for what follows – for once I'm thinking clearly and being very sensible.

I apologise if I ramble. All this stuff has been in my head since the other night, since our argument; and today more than ever. It's not fair on you that we keep on seeing each other. Let me explain my reasons. You want to enjoy yourself, see your friends, go shopping and clubbing, and I just get in your way. You're planning to go to university and have a great time next year – just like I did a couple of years ago.

There's nothing wrong with that. But that's not my world any more and I feel that I'm stopping you from doing all that stuff. I don't think I've got it in me to try to make conversation with Debbie and your other mates – we're from different worlds. I've got nothing to say to them and I don't think they'd like me. You understand me, but I don't think they would. It's not that I care what they think of me, just that I don't ever want you to feel that you have to apologise for me.

I feel like I've trespassed into your life. My only justification is the way I feel about you. I don't know if you feel the same, but even if you do, is that enough? You shouldn't have to make a choice between your friends and your work and me. It's not fair on you.

I'm ending our relationship now because every day I care for you more. Tomorrow, or the next day, I probably wouldn't be able to write this. I'm in so deep that if I go deeper I won't stay afloat without you. I care about you more than I have ever cared about anyone before. I love you. There, I've said it. I love you. And the more I love you, the more I want to be with you and only you.

It hurts to write this to you, but it must be written. If I tried to tell you to your face, or over the phone, it would all come out wrong. I'm putting my own feelings last to protect yours. Because you're the important one. Don't be angry that I'm making this decision on your behalf. I hope you understand. I want you to be happy, I want you to have a wonderful, successful life, with great friends. I don't want to hold you back. You are the most special person I have ever met. You deserve better than me.

I've gone on too long. I won't pick you up from work tomorrow. Don't come to rehearsal on Tuesday. Always remember the wonderful times we've shared and move on with your life.

Yours,
Danny x

I pulled myself upright, leaning on the door frame for support. The acid was rising from my stomach into my mouth and I thought I was going to vomit. I swallowed it down again, burning my throat and leaving an acrid taste in my mouth. From my first reading only five words had stayed with me, jumping out from the text and obscuring everything else: *I'm ending our relationship now.*

Danny was finishing with me. He was telling me he didn't want to see me again. He was leaving me. I was finding it hard to breathe, gasping for air, my ears filling with blood and a strange rushing sound. Was I having a heart attack? Was this what it was like to die? I tried to call out to my parents, but nothing came out of my mouth.

Focus, Naomi, focus, said a strange, calm voice inside my head. Although I had no control of my body, I managed to slump down into a sitting position. I closed my eyes and concentrated on breathing deeply, in and out, in and out. Then I read the letter again. This time different phrases leapt from the pages: *I love you. You are the most special person I have ever met.* Danny loved me. He loved me. So why was he dumping me? It didn't make sense. Because of Debbie? Because I was going to university in October? But I loved him too – didn't he realise? Didn't he understand that nothing and nobody else mattered? Now I was angry. How could he simultaneously tell me he loved me for the first time and finish with me? How could he make this decision on my behalf? Who did he think he was?

I dragged myself up again and opened the front door, drinking the cold, damp air into my lungs. I had only one purpose: whatever the outcome, I had to tell Danny that I loved him. He HAD to know. My legs started to run of their own accord, pulling my body with them. Soon I was running faster than I'd ever run before, past houses and across roads, dodging traffic and pedestrians, uphill, downhill, through puddles and muddy grass and around sharp bends. I'd never been a very good athlete – I even hated running for the bus – but adrenaline was pumping through my body and fuelling my muscles, propelling me forward. I had no sense of time or distance; I might have been running for five minutes or an hour, covering a hundred metres or a hundred miles.

I didn't stop running until I was standing outside Danny's front door, breathing so fast that I thought my lungs would explode. I pressed the doorbell and left my finger on it, making it scream continuously until somebody came to let me in. I didn't care what anybody thought, didn't mind if I was disturbing the peace. I would have stood there all night if I'd had to.

'What the hell is going on?' Danny's mother was standing at the door. When she saw me her expression changed from anger to shock to alarm. 'Are you all right, Naomi? You look terrible – you're soaked through. What's happened?'

I was still hyperventilating, tears streaming down my face, my jeans and coat splattered with mud. 'Please, I need to see Danny. Please . . .'

Shaking her head, she let me pass her, stepping away from me so, I assume, I didn't stain her pristine dress.

'Danny's in his flat,' she said. 'You know the way.'

I didn't thank her – I was already banging on his door.

He opened it almost immediately. 'Naomi?' he said, bewildered. He had dark circles under his eyes and it looked as if he hadn't shaved for a couple of days. 'What are you doing here?' His mother was still loitering in the hall, curious. He nodded at her. 'It's all right, Mum, you can go now. I'll deal with this.'

He led me into his flat, locking the door behind us. 'What are you doing here?' he asked again. His arm twitched in my direction and I could tell he wanted to touch me, but he wouldn't let himself.

'Your letter . . . I . . . how could you? I don't understand.' I began to sob, huge, chest-filling sobs, like hiccoughs that I couldn't control.

'Sit down,' he said. 'Sit down and have a drink and then we'll talk.'

He made me a cup of tea and watched as I sipped it. Soon I had stopped shaking and my sobs had begun to subside. Suddenly self-aware, I felt foolish and then worried about what I must look like, with my hair plastered to my face and no make-up.

'I'm sorry, Omi. I didn't mean to upset you like this,' said Danny gently.

'I don't understand,' I repeated. 'You tell me that you love me and then you finish it. It doesn't make sense.'

'It made sense to me when I wrote it. I thought it was for the best. It is for the best.'

'But why? What about how *I* feel? I love you too. I didn't know how to tell you, but I do. And—'

'You what?' he exclaimed, his eyes growing wider.

'I love you,' I muttered, embarrassed.

His eyes pierced into mine. 'You do?'

'Yes, of course.'

'Say it again,' he demanded.

'OK, I love you.'

'Again!'

I was almost laughing now. 'I love you.'

'Again!' he cried. 'You have no idea how much I've wanted to hear you say that.'

'I love you, Danny,' I told him, frustrated that I couldn't infuse those three syllables with the colour and depth that lay behind them. 'I love you, I love you.'

'That's amazing,' he said, shaking his head. 'I can't tell

you how happy you've made me.'

He walked over to me and took my hands, pulling me up from my chair. Then he wrapped his arms around my back and pulled me tight into his body, kissing me so hard and so urgently that I was momentarily afraid I might be swallowed whole. Soon I was kissing him back, channelling all the emotions within me – all the words I should have said and the thoughts I couldn't articulate – into kisses. I was kissing him with my body and my mind and my soul. After that kiss, there was no going back for me, no escape. Danny had me. He was no longer just my boyfriend, he was part of me. We were one entity: NaomiandDanny, DannyandNaomi.

We never spoke about the letter again. I regret that now. I should have asked him why he had turned a small argument into such a big drama. Did a little bit of him enjoy it? Had he foreseen the effect that letter would have on me – was it all part of a clever game? And, most importantly, why would he try to protect me from himself?

I didn't ask because I was so caught up in the intensity of his feelings, and mine. In my half-formed dictionary of love, D-R-A-M-A was spelled P-A-S-S-I-O-N. The sad thing is, even if I *had* asked, I don't think he'd have had the answers.

Chapter 11

D anny was on stage, singing to a crowd of about eighty people in a dingy room at the back of a pub. He had played in hundreds of venues just like it – dark, hot rooms that smelled of stale beer and cigarettes. But this night was different. Somewhere in the crowd stood an A&R man named Jed Wilson who had the power to change Danny's life forever. If he liked The Wonderfulls he could give them a record contract: the golden ticket that would take them out of local pubs, out of new band nights and poorly paid support slots, and put them on the bill at festivals and thousand-seater venues and even, one day, stadiums.

Danny wanted a record contract more than he wanted anything. There was no point fooling myself; no matter how much he declared that he loved me, if he'd had to choose between a record contract and me, I'm pretty sure I'd have been a poor runner-up. Music was his first love. Danny had spent his childhood imagining himself on stage at Wembley, a huge crowd mouthing along to his lyrics. Unlike most childhood dreams, which are drummed out of us by the realisation that we don't have the talent or the opportunity to fulfil them, Danny's had stayed with him, growing ever stronger. If you were to take away the deep

voice and the stubble and the six-foot stature, you'd see he
was still just a little boy playing air guitar in front of the
mirror.

'You'll be fantastic,' I reassured him, as we drove to the
venue for the soundcheck earlier that afternoon. 'The
record company would be mad not to sign you.' I knew it
was what he needed to hear and I wanted him to be successful because it meant so much to him. But part of me
feared what might happen if The Wonderfulls achieved
fame and fortune. Success would change him; it was
inevitable. Would there be room in his life for me, what
with recording sessions and tours and magazine interviews?
And what about all the girls he'd meet, groupies who were
prettier and more interesting than me?

No matter how much he told me that he loved me, that
I was beautiful and funny and clever, nothing could erase
the nagging doubt that I might not be good enough for him.
I felt I'd lucked out and that one day Danny would wake
up and realise that he'd made a mistake. I'd noticed the way
some of the girl fans looked at me, and I imagined them
whispering to their friends about my features or my figure,
asking, 'What's he doing with her?' I sometimes asked
myself the same question. I don't know where self-esteem
comes from – perhaps you're born with it. My lack of it
certainly wasn't my parents' fault; they'd always told me I
was pretty and special, that I could be anything I wanted to
be. It had just never seemed that way to me.

Seated at the side of the stage at a table covered in flyers
and demo CDs, I looked into the crowd and tried to work

out where Jed Wilson was standing. There were several men I didn't recognise, but they could equally have been there to see one of the other bands performing that night. Jed, I decided, would be alone and he'd probably be aloof and dressed a little too smartly, almost certainly in black. Danny had told me that most A & R men were terminally uncool, desperate to appear young and trendy and 'down with the kids', when in reality they were just overpaid businessmen heading towards middle age. There were a couple of guys who fitted the bill, one with a – presumably – 'ironic' mullet-type hairstyle and another whose jeans and T-shirt looked as though they might have been pressed. I watched them closely for a while; neither seemed to be enjoying himself much. If one of them was indeed Jed, it wasn't a good sign.

Although nobody would admit it openly, the band's rehearsals – which were disorganised at the best of times – had not been going well. Dylan had failed to turn up on several occasions and nobody had been able to contact him. Danny had taken his place, but the bass guitar wasn't his instrument and he'd found it hard to sing and play at the same time. When Dylan had finally resurfaced, he had offered few excuses for his absences and was not even apologetic. From his weary and unkempt demeanour it was obvious that he had been smoking far too much pot. He no longer seemed to care whether The Wonderfulls made it; he no longer cared about anything much at all. Worried that Dylan might leave altogether, the others kept their irritation to themselves, but the tension between them was palpable.

Still, the gig was as successful as anyone might hope. Danny was in fine voice, Dylan had got his act together and most of The Wonderfulls' fans had shown up to cheer them on. There had been a lot of buzz on the website about the possibility of a record deal and everybody appeared to like Danny's new songs. I watched the crowd's reactions as they heard them for the first time; they clapped and shouted their appreciation as much as they did for any of the old favourites. That gave me a warm feeling. I had seen the songs progress from scrawls in Danny's notebook to demos to full performances – I knew them as well as the band did. So when Danny said, 'This is a song for someone very special,' and looked directly at me, my heart leapt in to my mouth. I knew exactly what he was about to sing.

Not long after the letter incident, on Valentine's Day, Danny had sent me a cryptic text, inviting me to his flat that evening for 'a surprise'. I still found the idea of surprises rather unnerving but, since the picnic, I no longer dreaded them. I had no idea what it might be and I spent the whole day at work in a state of nervous excitement, imagining every possible scenario. He had already sent me a huge card and had flowers delivered to me at work – surprises enough, after he'd told me he thought Valentine's Day was just a commercial enterprise dreamed up by greeting card manufacturers. Foolishly, I'd taken him at his word and sent him nothing. Now I felt guilty and spoiled.

So what else did he have planned? Perhaps he was going to cook me a special meal, or present me with a gift, or even – if I let myself get carried away – whisk me off somewhere romantic, like Paris or Rome. Alone in the photocopying room I practised my reaction: a look of shock, followed by a tearful 'thank you'. As a child, I'd rehearsed my Oscar acceptance speech in much the same way, mouthing the words in the mirror and concentrating hard on sad things – in those days it was abandoned kittens – to conjure up genuine tears in my eyes. Now all I had to do was imagine not being with Danny.

I quickly changed in the toilets at work and took the bus straight to Danny's house, choosing a seat at the back so that nobody could watch me applying my make-up. When I arrived, he was standing in his drive waiting for me. I ran into his arms, letting him lift me up and cover my face with kisses.

'Are you ready for your surprise?' he asked. He was smiling, but he seemed a little agitated.

'Absolutely,' I replied, with as much enthusiasm as I could muster. His evident nerves had done nothing to calm my own.

He took my hand and led me into his flat, asking me to sit on the sofa while he disappeared into his bedroom to fetch my gift. When he came out he was carrying his guitar. For a moment, I thought, *He's giving me his guitar*, but it didn't make sense. He knew I couldn't really play and it was his prized possession. I tried hard not to look confused.

'OK,' he said. He hung back near the door. 'This is what I've been waiting to give you . . . I've written you a song. I hope you like it.'

Resting his leg on a footstool, he pulled his guitar strap

over his head and began to play a series of chords, which (thanks to years of school and Mum's music lessons) I could tell were in the key of G. He was so jittery that his fingers fumbled for the strings. Then he cleared his throat and, after a couple of false starts, he began to sing:

> 'Take it, take it now;
> This precious moment will allow
> Time to stop and heal all pain.
> You are the sun that halts the rain.
>
> And the dark clouds will disappear;
> You are the calm that quells my fear;
> Fate has cast the starring role,
> So take the stage and save my soul.
> Save my soul.
>
> Take my hand, take my hand.
> The best things in life are never planned.
> That captured smile, two worlds collide,
> My shooting star, my guiding light.
>
> You will always be
> The other half of me,
> And if my world should fall apart
> You would be there
> To mend my heart.'

When he had finished, he put down his guitar and leaned against the door frame, waiting for a reaction. I didn't know what to say. I felt I needed to hear the song again before I could compose my thoughts. I was still scrolling through the song's lyrics, seeing them lined up in my mind, as though they were written on a screen. Danny had said I was his other half, that I could save his soul – he had sung of being with me forever. He'd said things in song that would have sounded over the top, scary even, in plain speech. But somehow, as lyrics, they worked. Whatever I said in response would seem trite. I felt as if I wanted to write a song back to him to express my feelings, but I didn't know how. So I sat there, in silence, overwhelmed by the words and the music and Danny's incredible voice, trying to compute it all.

'You didn't like it,' he said, hanging his head in resignation. Danny always assumed the worst.

'No, no, I loved it!' I said, hoping the tone of my voice would convey the emotions I couldn't articulate. 'I really, really loved it. I'm just stunned. Did you really write that for me?'

'Of course I did,' he said, laughing. Now he was perky, like a dog that has just been petted. He came over to sit beside me. 'Who else?'

'Angelina Jolie, perhaps?' I joked. 'Honestly, Danny, it's the best present you could have given me.'

And it was. Nobody else in the world had ever received this present and nobody would again; it had been created just for me. I didn't ask Danny about the detail of the lyrics. To be honest, I was a little embarrassed by the intensity of them. Instead, I said the only thing I could think of that seemed appropriate and would please him. I said, 'I love you, Danny.'

Loving Danny

Ever since Danny and I had admitted that we loved one another, we hadn't been able to stop saying it. To me, the words 'I love you' were like a magic spell, and one which I was afraid would be broken if I didn't keep saying and hearing them. They made me tingle all over, sapped my appetite and cleared my mind of any other thoughts. They were also a useful silence-filler, a way to make up quickly if we disagreed, or to cheer each other up when we felt down. Now, as a response to Danny's song, they were shorthand for: 'Thank you, I'm not sure exactly what you're saying to me here, but, whatever it is, I feel the same.'

Hearing the song – *my* song – played at Danny's gig that night was just as special as the first time. It wasn't just because Danny looked deep into my eyes as he sang, sending warm shivers through my whole body. It was also because he was singing it in public – declaring his love for me in front of all his fans. Even though it was dark and the audience's attention was focused on the stage, I felt proud, as if all eyes were on me. I wondered if the crowd were listening to the words and imagining who they were about, who Danny's muse might be. I'd always envied girls who'd had songs written for them – they were usually beautiful models or actresses or tragic icons. How incredible that I, plain old Naomi Waterman, was now one of them. If The Wonderfulls made it big, 'my' song could be played on radios and CD players all over the world. How amazing would that be?

When he had finished singing the song and the whoops were building to a climax, Danny made a show of putting down his guitar and turning to walk off the stage. The others followed him. It's a ploy every band uses at the end of their set: whip the crowd up into a frenzy and then, when they are hoarse from cheering and tired from stomping and clapping, come back on stage to perform an encore. I often wondered what might happen if the crowd didn't behave as anticipated, and started walking out. But that night, as always, it worked a treat.

Two songs later, the lights came on to signal that the gig really was over. Danny threw down his guitar and jumped from the stage, rushing straight over to me. 'Is Jed here?' he said breathlessly. 'Did you see him?'

'I'm not sure,' I replied, looking back into the crowd, which was now dispersing. It was eleven o'clock and the pub staff were hurrying people to finish their drinks and leave the premises. There was no sign of mullet-man or the guy with pressed jeans. 'I thought I saw him earlier – or someone who might have been him,' I volunteered. 'I didn't notice him leave. Maybe he's in the loo or something?'

'Stay here,' said Danny. 'I'll just be a sec.'

He clambered back on stage and said something to a couple of the other band members. There was lots of head shaking and shoulder shrugging. Then he was off again, weaving his way through the crowd to find someone who might know the whereabouts of Jed Wilson. I saw him speaking to a guy I recognised from the website as one of The Wonderfulls' fans. I think he was called Simon. He was short and broad and his belly spilled over his jeans like milk boiling over from a pan. I watched as he gave Danny a bear hug, patting him on the back and whispering something into his ear. Danny gave him a quizzical look, then made his way back to me, deliberately dodging other fans, who had hung around to congratulate him on the gig. His body language had changed completely; he looked tired and dejected.

'He was here,' said Danny. 'But the bastard left halfway through the set, apparently.'

'That doesn't mean anything, does it?'

'Don't be naïve, Naomi. He obviously didn't dig us.'

'But you were great tonight. Really great.'

'Not great enough, it seems.'

'Maybe he'll give you a call tomorrow. Maybe he needed to talk to someone else first?'

'Maybe,' sighed Danny. 'But don't hold your breath. If he'd liked us, if he'd wanted to sign us, we'd know about it.'

I tried to hold his hand, but he brushed me away. When Danny was upset he found it hard to be affectionate. Seeing my hurt expression, he squeezed my shoulder and told me he'd meet me at the front of the pub once he'd helped the others to load up the equipment.

He drove in silence. He was deep in thought and I could tell he was torturing himself, wondering if he could have sung better or whether it was Dylan's fault, or if The Wonderfulls should have rehearsed more.

'There'll be other chances, Danny,' I said softly. 'I'm sure of it.'

'Maybe.'

I didn't want to leave him yet but he insisted on dropping me off at home. 'It's not you,' he promised. 'I won't be good company tonight. I want to be on my own. Come round tomorrow afternoon?'

'You were supposed to be coming for lunch, with my parents,' I reminded him.

'Oh shit. Look, can you tell them I'm really sorry. Make something up – I just don't feel like it, OK?'

'OK,' I said, disappointed. 'I'll come round after lunch, then.'

'That would be nice.' He smiled, sadly. I kissed him and for a moment he forgot himself and started to respond. But then he pulled away from me and leaned over to open the car door.

'I love you, Danny,' I said, hoping it might make him feel better.

'I love you too, Omi.' His voice was monotone.

Danny seemed in better spirits the next afternoon. He greeted me with a long, tender kiss, as if to make up for his lack of affection the previous night. 'I'm OK,' he assured me. 'I've had a chat with the others and we're going to record some more demos and send them out. We won't let the bastards get us down.'

I had told my parents that he'd missed lunch because he didn't feel very well and that I was going over later to look after him. They'd accepted my explanation without too much fuss and didn't question me further. Mum had even let me off dessert and asked, with genuine concern, if Danny needed anything. I'd almost quipped, 'A record deal,' but thought better of it.

We lounged around on Danny's sofa for a couple of hours, listening to music and watching rubbish television. I was always amazed how much trivia Danny kept in his head. He knew all the characters' names in the soaps, what the actors had been in before and what was going on in their private lives. But he was also well up on current affairs, able to fill me in on the latest developments in the Middle East and why a particular economic policy was bad news for the country. As for his knowledge of music, it was encyclopaedic. Whenever I said I liked a particular song, he'd say, 'You might like this, then,' and he'd go to his CD collection – which covered the wall of his living room – and pick out something by an obscure artist I'd never heard of. He was the same with books. His brain was like a sponge – if he was interested in something he had to know it all, to possess it.

'Do you fancy doing something – going somewhere, maybe?' I asked when the central heating began to make me feel drowsy.

'Sure,' he said. 'We could go into town, do a museum or gallery or something.'

I nodded. 'That would be nice.'

'I'd better get changed,' he said. He was wearing last night's long-sleeved, grey T-shirt, which now smelled of stale smoke and sweat. I watched as he peeled it over his head, admiring his slim torso and muscular shoulders. But as he pulled off the sleeves, I noticed a large, flesh-coloured plaster on his forearm. It hadn't been there yesterday.

'What happened to your arm, Danny?' I was curious and a little concerned.

'Hey?' His head was still caught on the top. He wriggled out of it.

'The plaster. Did you hurt yourself?'

He became suddenly modest, draping the T-shirt over himself and avoiding eye contact. 'Oh, that. It's nothing. I caught myself on a guitar string last night. Don't worry about it.'

But I was worried. I knew Danny well enough by now to know when he was lying. It seemed odd – more than coincidence, certainly – that a guitar string should have cut him on almost the same part of his arm as his old, school-boy injury. Or, maybe that hadn't been an accident either. Could he have done it to himself? Were both wounds self-inflicted? Were they drug-related? Was Danny doing more than just smoking the odd spliff? Or had he been in a fight?

Before I could say anything else, Danny had scurried into the bedroom. When he returned, his top changed, he was smiling. 'Let's go, then.'

'All right,' I said, forcing myself to smile back.

I brushed my worries to the back of my mind – I was getting good at that. I hated myself for feeling suspicious of Danny and anyway, it didn't make sense. People only hurt themselves or picked fights when they were really troubled or depressed, didn't they? Last night hadn't gone well, but Danny didn't generally seem down, did he? If Danny was doing something destructive, it could only mean that there was something he wasn't telling me . . . that I wasn't making him happy. Didn't he feel close enough to me to confide in me? Wasn't I enough for him? Might it even be my fault? I couldn't face that possibility; it was far better for me to ignore my concerns and play dumb. I wasn't yet ready to open Pandora's box.

We caught the bus into town and walked around for a while, looking in the shop windows. Then we went to see a photographic exhibition, which I'd mentioned I fancied catching. I'd never had anyone to go to this type of exhibition with before – my friends thought them boring. But Danny encouraged my love of photography; he said I was talented and should dump law and make a career out of it. I was starting to think that it was a good idea. Danny had a lot of good ideas. They took me down avenues I'd never have visited on my own and made me aware that, if I wanted, I could skirt around the paths that I felt had been laid out for me.

Chapter 12

Danny dropped me home late that night. I walked through the front door, smiling to myself, feeling that I was wrapped in the warm glow of happiness. I'd had a lovely time with Danny at the exhibition and we had followed it with a meal out and a hot chocolate back at his place.

But as I entered the hall I noticed that the kitchen light was on. I peered around the door to find Mum and Dad sitting at the kitchen table, waiting for me.

'Where have you been?' asked Dad in a nagging voice, which I knew meant trouble.

'You know where I've been – I've been at Danny's.' I was still smiling. 'We went to an exhibition – I've got some postcards – look.' I rummaged around in my bag. I'd bought some great images, portraits that had been taken using this cool technique called solarisation, which made them look like paintings. I was really excited by it.

'I thought he was ill,' said Mum, obviously hurt that I had lied.

I cursed myself silently for forgetting. Mum had seemed genuinely concerned about Danny and now I'd disappointed her and dropped him in it too. 'He was feeling better,' I said. I quickly changed the subject. 'Anyway, why are you up so late – isn't it past your bedtime?' I grinned, checking my watch. It was almost one in the morning.

'This is not the time to be cheeky,' said Dad flatly. 'We've been at a charity supper quiz. I'm sure that doesn't interest you. But what you might like to know is that Martin Stevens was there.'

'Oh.' Martin Stevens was, of course, my boss and an acquaintance of Dad's. 'How was he?'

'He was absolutely fine and so was his wife. However, he's under the impression that *you* haven't been too well of late.'

'Really?' I asked.

I hadn't expected the attack, wasn't prepared for it.

'You know exactly what I'm talking about, Naomi, don't deny it. Martin said you've had a few days off here and there, without notice, and that you've been coming in late rather too often. He's also noticed that you're not performing very well, that your mind doesn't seem to be on the job. Have you got anything to say to that?'

'No, not really,' I muttered.

'Well, is it true?'

'I guess, a bit.'

'Why, Naomi? You worked so hard to get that placement and it took no small amount of effort on my part, either. Why are you letting yourself down?'

'It's boring,' I said. 'It's not what I expected at all. They leave me alone half the day, doing stuff like filing and photocopying. I hate it.'

'What did you expect? You're hardly likely to be asked to represent people in court now, are you? For heaven's sake, Naomi, this is an opportunity to learn about how things work, to get some experience for your CV. It's invaluable for your degree and it could potentially lead to future work as a lawyer in that practice.'

'I'm not sure I want to be a lawyer,' I said quietly.

'Pardon?'

'I don't think I want to work in law after all.'

Dad got up from the table. 'What? You are joking, aren't you? You've got a place at one of the best universities in the country to read law next year and now you say you've changed your mind?'

'Yes,' I said. 'I've changed my mind. I'm going to pack in law and do photography instead. Danny thinks I'm a natural.' As I said it I thought, *Yes, that's what I want to do. I'll become a photographer.* Saying the words helped shaped the idea in my mind, made it a real option.

Dad exploded. 'You nincompoop!' It was such a funny word that I had to try hard not to laugh. Dad was always so worried about not swearing that he kept a collection of the most old-fashioned expressions in his head. He was the only person I knew who still said 'crikey' and 'good grief' and 'gosh'. 'Nincompoop' was his favourite when he thought someone was acting like an idiot. 'You fool!' he continued. 'After all your years of hard work you're now planning on throwing it all away. I'm very disappointed, Naomi. Very disappointed. You're just being ... stupid!' His round face was red and puffy with anger, his cheeks swelling like a cooked tomato that was about to explode.

'I'm not being stupid!' I shouted. 'I'm just doing what I want for a change.'

'Are you?' interrupted Mum, in a calm, soft voice. She had kept quiet until now. She got up from the table and walked over to my side.

'Of course. What do you mean?'

'Are you doing what you really want or what Danny wants you to do?'

'They're the same thing,' I said. 'Danny knows me. He understands me.'

'But you never said you wanted to do photography before. You always had your heart set on becoming a lawyer.'

'I've always enjoyed photography, you know I have.'

'Yes, as a hobby, not a career. It just strikes me that it's Danny who's encouraged this. He's a nice, intelligent boy and we like him very much, but he has some crazy ideas.'

'What's crazy about photography?'

'That's not what I mean. We're not wealthy like Danny's family. We can't support you forever. We want you to have a career that will give you a happy, comfortable life. I don't think you've thought this through, Naomi. Have you?'

She was right. I hadn't. But I wasn't going to let her know that.

'Yes, I have. It's what I want to do and if you won't support me, that's fine. Danny will be there for me.'

'Don't be ridiculous!' Dad spluttered. 'You're eighteen

years old, he's – what – twenty? You might both feel differently in a few years. Do you really think life is that easy?'

That hurt. I'd believed that Mum and Dad knew how serious I was about Danny. Now it transpired that they thought it was just a silly, teenage fling.

'But I love him,' I said. 'And he loves me. We're soulmates.'

'Oh, Naomi,' said Mum. She came towards me and tried to hug me, but I left my arms hanging by my sides. 'I know you love him. But love doesn't pay the bills.'

'We'll work something out,' I said.

Mum tried another tack. 'Naomi, do you think that you would have changed your mind about law if it hadn't been for Danny?'

'I don't know,' I said. 'Maybe.'

She was hesitant. 'You know we like Danny . . . it's just that you seem to have been very influenced by him.'

'Influenced?'

'Yes. Ever since you started going out with him you've done nothing but talk about him and his band. You haven't seen any of your other friends – you hardly speak to Debbie any more. Now we find out you've missed work too. And today, you lied for him. He's a very strong character. Where have you gone, Naomi?'

'This is me,' I said, pointing to my chest. 'This is the real me. Maybe I just didn't realise it before.'

Mum shook her head in exasperation. 'We're not trying to upset you, we're just worried about you. We don't want you to make any foolish mistakes.'

'I thought you liked him. You said you liked him!'

'We do, Naomi. But he doesn't seem the most responsible or stable person.'

She had touched a raw nerve, questioned the very things that had begun to worry me about Danny. Rather than admit that – to Mum or to myself – I reacted with anger. 'What?! I'm eighteen, I don't want stability or responsibility. You're so middle-aged.'

'Don't be rude to your mother,' said Dad protectively. 'We've got more life experience than you and we can see that you're risking making a mistake. Maybe you should take some time out for yourself ... perhaps you should stop seeing Danny for a while, eh?'

'No!' I cried. I looked at Mum, pleading with my eyes. Surely she must understand. 'You can't ask me to do that. I love him.'

'I think it's for the best,' she said flatly, her eyes downcast. 'Just for a little bit, while you have a think about things.'

I couldn't believe what I was hearing. She wasn't my rational, kind, understanding mother – she must be an alien replicant. She knew how happy Danny made me. How could she ask me to break up with him?

'I can't do it!' I shouted. 'I won't do it.'

'Can't do what?' None of us had noticed that Emily had wandered into the room. She was wearing her nightie and looked bleary-eyed.

'It's nothing, Emily,' said Mum. 'Go back to bed. You've got school in the morning.'

Emily didn't move. 'I woke up and heard raised voices,' she said, looking from Mum to Dad to me and then back to Mum again. 'Has something happened?'

'No,' said Mum. 'It's all OK.'

'Yes!' I cried, certain that Emily would understand and take my side. 'It's not OK. Mum and Dad want me to stop seeing Danny.'

Emily walked over to me and placed her hand on my shoulder. '*What*? Why?'

'They think he's a bad influence.'

Mum sighed. 'That's not exactly what we said, Naomi. We just said things were getting a bit out of hand and that maybe you should take some time to think about it all.'

I could feel my face growing red, the muscles in my jaw and forehead clenching. I stepped forward, unsure what I would do or say, my arms flailing in frustration.

'I'm sure there's another way,' said Emily, stroking my hair. She chewed her lip in thought. She had taken it upon herself to play the mediator. 'Naomi loves Danny – she's been so happy since she met him. Can't you give him another chance and then see?'

'For heaven's sake,' said Dad, irritated. 'This is getting silly. What we have suggested is very sensible – some time apart for Naomi to sort herself out.'

'I can't do it,' I repeated.

'It might not be your choice. You live under our roof,' said Dad firmly. I didn't like his insinuation.

'I'm eighteen, I'm an adult. If you don't want me to see Danny, I'll leave home.'

Dad laughed. 'And where exactly will you go?'

'To Danny's,' I stated. My hand was already reaching for the mobile phone in my coat pocket. 'I'm going to go round there now.'

'It's the middle of the night,' said Mum. I could tell she was anxious, worried that she and Dad had gone too far.

'Don't be silly, Nay,' said Emily. She tried to stroke my hair again, but I pushed her hand away. Her bottom lip began to quiver. I felt awful. She hated it when anybody argued and here she was, right in the middle of it, trying to appease all three of us and getting nowhere. 'Why don't you sleep on it and when everybody's calmed down we'll talk about it some more?' she added, her voice shaky.

I mulled over Emily's idea. 'Will you change your mind about Danny?' I asked Dad.

'Of course not,' he said stubbornly.

'Well, in that case, there's no point.' I started walking into the hall. I felt strangely exhilarated. 'I'm not going to change my mind about him either. So I might as well go now.'

'Naomi!' Mum shouted. 'Don't be silly. Come back!'

'Please don't go, Nay,' begged Emily, as tears began to roll down her face.

I was aware that she was following close behind me, but I didn't turn around – I quickened my pace. As I slammed the front door behind me I heard Mum and Emily still calling, 'Naomi! Naomi!'

I phoned Danny from the corner of my road. I prayed

he was not yet asleep and would pick up. I hid myself behind a hedge, in case my parents came out looking for me. Going home was not an option – I had left my keys in the hall and I couldn't face Mum and Dad's smug looks if I rang the doorbell in defeat. We'd never fallen out like this before and I wanted them to know how important Danny was to me. I was desperately upset, and not quite sure what I was doing, but one thing was certain – they deserved to sweat a little.

Thankfully, Danny answered the phone immediately.

'Please come and get me,' I sobbed, before he could say a word.

'What's happened, Omi? Are you OK? Where are you?'

'I'm at the end of my street. Please come and get me, Danny.'

'Of course I will,' he said, the tone of his voice coloured by a mixture of reassurance, confusion and concern. 'Give me five minutes.'

It seemed to take forever for Danny to arrive. Standing there, waiting alone in the darkness, I felt cold and vulnerable. Every time I heard the sound of a car I stepped out from the shadows, allowing myself to be illuminated by its headlights. None of them was Danny's. One car slowed down, causing my heart to beat wildly in terror. *All I need now*, I thought, *is to be abducted by some crazed sex attacker. My parents would think I was with Danny and nobody would report me missing for days.*

Loving Danny

I recognised the sound of Danny's engine before I saw his car. For once I was pleased that he was speeding up my road; sod the speed limit – it meant he cared. As he screeched to a stop he flung open the passenger door for me.

'What's happened?' he asked again. I was shaking with cold, fear and anger and he looked panic-stricken.

'Oh Danny, I'm so pleased to see you!' I cried, leaning over and flinging my arms around him. 'Please take me back to your flat. I don't want my parents to see me.'

He clasped me so tightly that I couldn't breathe. 'For God's sake, what's happened?'

'It's my parents. We had a row. They don't want me to see you any more.'

'What?' he said, loosening his grip. 'I don't under-stand.'

'Nor do I,' I said. 'They think you're a bad influence.'

'What? I thought they liked me?'

'Please drive, Danny.'

'OK, but will you please tell me what's going on?'

As we drove I told Danny about how Dad had bumped into Martin Stevens and the argument it had caused. He listened intently, his expression growing stony cold with anger.

'Your idiot parents don't know what they're talking about,' he said. There was no longer concern in his voice, only indignation and spite.

'I think they mean well,' I said, trying to placate him. Angry as I was, I didn't like to hear him talk about my parents so hatefully. He didn't know them well enough to judge them. 'They're just overreacting.'

'They're trying to control your life, more like. What right have they to tell you not to see me?'

'None, Danny,' I said. 'They can't make me break up with you.'

'Damn right, they can't. I hope you told them that.'

'Of course I did. I don't think they believed it when I walked out.' I managed a shaky little laugh at my own gall. 'I've never done anything like this before.'

'Well, maybe you should have. You've let them push you around for too long. They don't understand you like I do – they're just trying to turn you into a clone of them. Listen, Omi, as far as I'm concerned, you can stay at mine as long as you like. Sod your parents.'

'Thanks,' I said, still uncomfortable with the way he was slating my parents. I was angry with them, sure, but they had their good points, and when it came down to it, I loved them. Why were Danny's emotions always so extreme? He saw everything in black and white. 'Maybe they'll calm down by the morning,' I suggested.

'It's already the morning,' Danny reminded me.

I looked at my watch. 'Damn, I'm due in the office in less than seven hours.'

'You hate that job. Why not pack it in right now? You don't want to be a lawyer anyway.'

'I need the money, Danny.'

'I've got enough money for both of us. I'll see you right.'

'Thanks, Danny, but I'm not sure.' I thought on the spot. 'I'm due a week off anyway. I'll call in tomorrow and tell them I need a few days' break now.'

'Great,' he said. 'We'll have a lovely time, you and me. Just you wait and see.'

Chapter 13

We did have a lovely time – for the first few days, at least. Being at Danny's, away from my parents and the stifling environment of my home, gave me a sense of freedom; it was like being on holiday. Arranging a break from work had been no trouble. By the time I called in – at ten o'clock on the morning after I'd left home – it was evident that Dad had already been in touch with Mr Stevens to smooth the way. He came on the line and, in a rather fatherly manner, told me that the practice had agreed to give me a couple of weeks leave 'to get your head together'. After that, I should come in to discuss my future. I had no idea whether or not I would go back; I honestly didn't care one way or the other.

It felt strange staying in such a big house, with its gated drive and huge garden. It could not have been more different from my house, where the walls and ceilings were thin and everybody knew each other's business. Danny's parents' house was so vast and so quiet; once I was shut safely away in his flat, there could have been a party going on in the main house and I wouldn't have known about it. I still hadn't met Mr Evans – he was away on another business trip – but Mrs Evans made me nervous and I dreaded bumping into her in the hall. Ever since our first meeting, when I'd almost knocked over her precious vase, she'd made me feel awkward and clumsy. And because she expected me to be clumsy, I succeeded in acting like it, tripping over my feet and banging into things whenever she was around me. When she spoke to me, I stuttered. It's funny how someone else's perception of you can have such a strong, unconscious effect on the way you behave.

Emily brought some of my stuff round on the second evening. She told me Mum was waiting in the car outside, so she couldn't stay long.

'She's really worried about you,' she said. 'Talk to her, Nay.'

'I can't. I'll ring her when I'm ready.'

'It's horrible at home. Mum and Dad have been arguing and dinner time is worse than ever. Come home, Nay. I'm sure you can sort things out.'

'I want to be with Danny,' I said, trying to sound stronger than I felt. 'Until Mum and Dad accept that, I'm staying put.'

Emily shrugged. She looked so sad that I felt guilty. I hadn't meant to make everybody miserable. As much as I loved being with Danny, I knew I wouldn't feel completely happy or settled until I had made things right with my parents.

After Emily had left I went downstairs to see Danny. He'd given me a key to his flat, but I still felt that I had to knock before I went in. Every time I did it he laughed at me. 'I do wish you'd chill out, Omi. The only person who knocks is the cleaning lady. Make yourself at home.'

'Sorry, Danny, I can't help it.'

'Stop apologising,' he said, playfully squeezing my cheeks. 'You seem really tense. What is it?'

'Oh, you know, it's just Emily coming round and thinking about all that stuff with my parents.'

'Your bloody parents again,' he hissed, rolling his eyes. Then, seeing that he had hurt me, his expression brightened. 'I just love having you here, Omi. I really hope you'll stay forever. Just you and me.'

He kissed me and everything felt better, instantly.

At first, Danny treated me like a princess, cooking me breakfast and dinner and generally fussing around me. He'd take me out wherever I wanted to go and buy me presents, like perfume and sweets. He even decided to take it upon himself to teach me to play the guitar, declaring me a natural when I mastered two chords at our first lesson. I'd never spent so much time with one person and I was surprised to find that we never irritated each other or ran out of things to talk about.

If I let myself ignore the situation with my parents, and the fact that this set-up could only be temporary, I could pretend that this was what it was like to be grown up and living with someone. Even mundane things, like going to the supermarket with Danny, made me feel closer to him. We'd walk down the aisles, hand in hand, and when other shoppers looked at us I felt proud because we were 'a couple' and everyone knew it.

But for Danny, at least, the novelty of having me around

soon wore off. By Wednesday he had already started to lapse into his old routines and I found myself having to fit into them. Danny liked to spend a lot of time alone, strumming his guitar or reading in silence. I hadn't realised before how lazy he was; he rarely got up before twelve and he didn't go out until nightfall unless he had to. If I tried to wake him early he'd be grumpy and tetchy, so I learned to amuse myself until I knew it was safe to talk to him. I watched hours of morning television, painted my nails and practised guitar chords on an old acoustic that he had lent me. By the end of the first week, however, the lessons had all but dried up; it appeared that Danny had run out of patience for teaching me.

I didn't want to admit it to myself, but I was starting to feel bored and, strangely, lonely. I couldn't help wondering if Danny might be growing tired of me, and each time that thought crossed my mind I felt sick and panicky. I tried to come up with ways of making him fall in love with me again, dressing up in the clothes he liked best and taking time to do my hair and make-up. I even wrote myself lists of amusing anecdotes that I knew might make him laugh, so that I could reel them off at a moment's notice and he'd remember how much fun we had together.

But for every moment that I feared Danny might have cooled towards me, there was another when his words and actions suggested that he loved me as much as ever. Sometimes, he would gaze into my eyes and tell me how special I was, how much he needed me. He would start writing a song and tell me that I had inspired it, that having me around was making him more creative than ever. Or he'd present me with a gift or make me a fabulous meal for no reason at all. His behaviour was so erratic that I didn't know whether I was coming or going. Was I doing or saying something wrong sometimes to make him cross with me? Could it be something of which I wasn't even conscious?

If only I had been honest with myself I would have realised that I was not the problem – Danny was. And it wasn't only me – he no longer seemed to be absorbed by anything for long. The new demos he had talked about The Wonderfulls making never materialised and very few gigs were lined up. Band rehearsals still took place in his flat, but lately they were more shambolic than ever. Only half the band would turn up at any one time, so they couldn't ever get any real playing done. Instead, whoever had made it on that particular night would jam with Danny for a while, and then they'd get a takeaway and some six-packs of beer and sit around getting stoned until they crashed out.

I felt even more of a spare part than before. I've never been the sort of girl who's 'one of the lads' and Danny's mates made it perfectly clear that I was in the way. One evening, when I was in the kitchen getting myself a drink, I overheard Andy referring to me as 'her indoors' and then laughing. Danny didn't really defend me, he just laughed and told Andy I was 'no trouble'. I was hurt, but I couldn't show it. Was that what Danny really thought of me? Or was he just being blokey in front of his mates? Too upset to put on a front, I excused myself and went to bed. And by the next day, it was forgotten. Danny was in such a sweet, affection-ate mood that I chose not to say anything.

On an icy Monday afternoon, a week after I'd arrived, I asked Danny if I could borrow his laptop to work on the band's website. It hadn't been updated for a while and I was worried that the fans would begin to lose interest if there wasn't some new hype for them to talk about. He seemed reluctant to get it for me.

'Don't bother, Omi,' he said. 'There's nothing new to put up.'

'Yeah, but it's good to change it a bit anyway. I've got some pictures I haven't used.'

'If you can be arsed.'

'Danny . . .' I began, gently, worried about his reaction to the question I was about to ask. 'Is everything all right with The Wonderfulls? It's just since the gig, since you didn't get signed, you've seemed like you don't really care any more.'

'Of course I care,' he replied, turning away from me. I realised that he looked tired, older even, his eyes hollow and his skin blotchy.

'Yes, but you're not really playing or rehearsing. You were going to record some demos, get some more interest . . . You haven't even finished any new songs.'

'Musician's block,' he muttered. 'It happens.'

'Maybe I could help?'

He laughed at me. 'What, with your two chords?'

'That's cruel.' My mouth fell into an involuntary pout. I emphasised it comically so he wouldn't know how much his comment had hurt me. It was his fault that I hadn't pro- gressed with the guitar; he was a poor teacher. Playing came instinctively to Danny – he couldn't explain things clearly, had little patience when I complained that my fingertips were hurting and he had simply stopped bothering to teach me. I could have said, 'You're the one who gives up if things don't come easy, not me.' But I didn't want to fight.

'Yes, it is cruel,' he said, smiling apologetically. 'Look, I'm sorry, but you don't know what you're talking about.'

'Maybe not,' I continued, feeling the frustrations of the past few days welling up inside me. 'But I do know that sitting around drinking and getting stoned with your waste-of-space mates isn't going to help.' The instant the words were out, I knew I'd sounded just like my mother.

Danny sneered. 'Get off your high horse, Naomi. Sometimes you can be so prissy. If you don't like it, you can get back to your boring friends and oh-so-middle-class parents and your law firm.'

I flinched. The flip side of knowing someone intimately is that they recognise exactly which buttons to press to hurt you, and Danny had gone too far now. I was no longer prepared to pussyfoot around him. If he wanted a fight, he could have one. 'You know what?' I spat. 'Maybe I will.'

'Go on, then. If you don't want to be here with me, then go.'

He looked me dead in the eye, daring me to get up and walk out. I knew he didn't think I would actually do it. He expected me to crumble, to apologise and to ask him to hold me and kiss me until our disagreement was forgotten. But I couldn't bring myself to do that. I was angry, and, more to the point, I was in the right. Wasn't I?

Realising that I'd talked myself into a corner, there was nothing for it but to act on my words. I may not be someone who relishes confrontation, but I'm no walkover. I stood up, marched to the door, and, without turning back to look at Danny, I opened it and slammed it behind me. Then I grabbed my coat and my gloves and left the flat as quickly as I could. I was panicking slightly – I didn't have any idea where I would go; I didn't have my phone with me, so I couldn't call anyone, and home certainly wasn't an option. *My parents would love it*, I thought, *if I'd turned up, my tail between my legs, with nowhere else to go.* There was no way I wanted to give them that satisfaction.

For about ten minutes or so, I just walked, letting my feet take me wherever they wanted to go. The streets around Danny's house were unfamiliar and I worried that I might become lost. But I soon came upon a landmark that I recognised: the gates of the park where Danny and I had spent our second date. It seemed apt that I had found my way to this park, with its happy memories; it was as though I had been meant to find it.

There were very few people about, just a couple of dog-walkers and some young boys playing football. Walking alone in a wide-open space just a couple of hours before nightfall probably wasn't the most sensible idea, but that didn't occur to me. I felt safe in that park, protected by the same trees and the same grass that had hosted my lovely picnic with Danny only four months earlier. If I listened carefully I could almost hear our laughter still echoing in the breeze. Everything had been so simple then, before other people – and real life – had intervened.

I headed for the playground and, ignoring the sign that read *Under-12s Only*, sat down on one of the swings. My eighteen-year-old bottom was too wide for it and the metal joints dug into my flesh, making me wince. It didn't seem fair to me that only children were supposed to go on the swings. I had never grown out of it. I still loved the sensation of freedom – flying through the air, reaching higher and higher with each kick of my legs, my hair flowing behind me and the wind on my face, until I was in danger of going over the top. As soon as I had my own place with a garden, I decided, I would install a swing – just for me.

As I swung, my anger dissipated. I wondered if Danny would come looking for me. Surely he must have realised that I wouldn't have gone home and maybe he, too, would be drawn here. I imagined him coming up behind me and pushing me on the swing, refusing to stop until we were both laughing so much that we had forgotten what we had argued about.

But he didn't come. After an hour, I decided to return to his flat. In my mind, I knew exactly how the conversation would go: I planned to tell him that I was sorry and that I knew it wasn't my place to interfere in The Wonderfulls. Then he would apologise too, tell me he wanted me to stay and we'd kiss and make up. In my eagerness to create a perfect end to a horrible day, I'd forgotten that conversations never seem to pan out quite the way you've planned them.

Chapter 14

Danny's flat was unexpectedly dark and oddly quiet when I let myself back in. It made me wonder if he had gone out looking for me, but his car was still in the drive and his favourite leather jacket was hanging from a hook in the hall. I had never known the flat to be silent; Danny always had some sort of music playing – there was a stereo system or radio in every room bar the toilet. He also had a habit of leaving the light on in each room he entered, so the place was always well lit. I couldn't put my finger on it, but there was a peculiar atmosphere in the flat, the darkness as eerie as the silence.

Something – an instinct, a sixth sense perhaps – stopped me from calling out Danny's name or switching on the lights myself. With my coat still buttoned up, I made my way first into the kitchen and then into the living room. There was no trace of Danny in either room, no coffee cups, plates or papers providing any evidence of recent activity. He must be in his bedroom, I thought. But the door was shut tight and I could hear no movement behind it. Had Danny gone to bed? He couldn't have. It was only a few hours since he had got up. Was he ill? What could he be doing in there?

I grasped the handle and pushed the door, letting it open a fraction. 'Danny?' I said softly. 'Are you in there?' There was no response. I peered through the crack, tentatively pushing the door a little further. In the faint light I could just make out a shape, a human form in front of me on the floor. 'Danny?' Again, no answer. With my heart hammering against my chest, I inched my way closer. Now I could see that the figure was hunched over, its head between its legs, rocking gently back and forth. 'Danny, are you OK?' The figure began to whimper, its breathing laboured and wheezy. 'Danny, what's happened?' Still there was no reply.

'I'm going to turn the light on, OK?'

'OK,' he croaked.

I paused before I pressed the light switch, nervous at the thought of what I might see. But nothing I had imagined could have prepared me for the sight that met my eyes. Danny was crouched on the carpet, his arms folded around his lowered head, his knees pulled into his chest. He was shaking like a young bird that has fallen from its mother's nest. It made no sense to me, but his jeans were splattered with what appeared to be red paint, and there was a small pool of paint by his feet.

Then I saw the kitchen knife, lying just a metre away from Danny, and I knew that it wasn't paint; it was blood.

Danny's blood.

I thought I was going to be sick. My first instinct was to flee from the room, to run outside and pretend that this had never happened, but I couldn't move. I was cemented to the carpet, my legs numb and heavy, as if they were encased in a plaster cast. Seconds passed. I began to count: one . . . two . . . three . . .

Loving Danny

'Oh my God, Danny, what have you done?' It was my voice, but it didn't belong to me – the words seemed to come from someone else's lips. The need to be practical had taken me over, it was driving me to action. I could feel the adrenaline coursing through my body, bringing my legs back to life and making my brain work in double time. Before I knew it I was at Danny's side, my arms around his back. 'Where are you hurt? Show me, Danny, show me.'

He looked up at me, his eyes watery and vacant. He opened his mouth, as if he were about to speak, and then closed it again. Then he sat up and unfolded his arms, and I could see that his left arm was wrapped in a makeshift bandage. He pointed to it. 'Here,' he said in a flat voice. 'Here.'

'Can I look?' I asked. He nodded. Afraid that I would hurt him, I unrolled the bandage as carefully as I could, praying that the bleeding had stopped. Part of the fabric had stuck to the wound and he winced as I pulled it away.

There were three gashes on his arm, two of them just scratches, but the third a long, deep slice in his flesh. The whole of his forearm was covered in dark, congealed blood. I didn't know anything about first aid, but I reasoned that if the bleeding had stopped it meant he didn't need stitches. He began to sob, deep, throaty sobs that made it difficult to catch his breath.

'I'm sorry, Omi, I'm so sorry,' he whimpered.

'It's OK, Danny, it's going to be OK,' I said. 'I'm here now.'

I fetched the first-aid kit from the bathroom cabinet and cleaned his wounds with antiseptic, bandaging them up again as best I could. Danny let me tend to him in silence, sitting still on the floor until I had finished. All his strength had gone; he was limp, like a giant baby.

When I had helped him change and put his clothes in the washing machine, I made him a cup of tea and told him to lie on the sofa and sip it slowly. I wished I'd made one for myself too. Now that the shock had passed I felt exhausted and my head was beginning to throb. I wanted to go to sleep, but I knew that I couldn't. I sat quietly for a while, Danny's head in my lap, trying to summon up the courage to talk about what had happened. The bloodstain on the bedroom carpet glared up at me through the open door and I knew that later I would have to get down on my hands and knees and scrub it away.

'It wasn't an accident, was it, Danny?' I asked, eventually, stating the obvious. We were now sitting side by side on the sofa, not quite touching. The inch of space between us felt like a yard. He shrugged and nodded.

'And the scars on your arm from before, they weren't an accident either?'

'No,' he said, hanging his head. He wouldn't meet my gaze.

So my half-formed suspicions, my instincts had been right. And yet, having them confirmed brought me no comfort, no relief at all, only more questions.

'I don't understand, Danny. Please help me understand.'

'It makes me feel better.'

'How?' I stroked his hair, as much to have something to do with my hands as to comfort him.

'It's hard to explain.' He sighed. 'It's like – when everything's getting to me, when I'm angry or upset – it makes the pain go away.'

'But doesn't it hurt?'

'No ... yes ... it's different. It hurts in a good way, because I'm making it happen. It's a buzz. And when the blood comes, it's like a release, it's like all my problems are draining away.'

'I don't understand. Is it my fault, Danny? Did I make you do it?'

'No,' he said, his voice cracking with frustration. Still, he wouldn't look at me. 'No, Omi, it's not you. You make everything better. When I'm around you I don't want to do it, I don't need to do it. Today, things just got out of control. I'm sorry, I'm really, really sorry.'

'It's OK,' I said, putting my arms around him. But it wasn't OK.

'I love you, Omi,' he whispered. He allowed me to hug him, but his arms remained limply in his lap.

'And I love you.'

Those three little words again. What did they mean, exactly? Speaking them required the same amount of breath, the same coordination of my lips and tongue as it had a thousand times before. They still sounded the same, were spelled the same. And yet, the words were now sticky with Danny's blood – imbued with a heaviness, a significance that they hadn't possessed before. What had I taken on by saying them? Only one thing was certain: I was in over my head. Way, way over my head.

Chapter 15

By the next morning Danny was his usual self again. He didn't want to talk about what had happened the day before – he seemed embarrassed about it, ashamed even – and he made me promise not to tell anyone. I agreed, reluctantly. I couldn't help feeling that *somebody* else should know. Fear, concern, pity, love, insecurity and a thousand other emotions I couldn't even name all swirled round and round in my head, swamping me like quicksand. I still couldn't comprehend what he had done; it made no sense. And if I didn't understand, how could I help him?

He larked around all day, telling me stupid jokes and trying to engage me in play fights, wrestling me on the sofa and then tickling me until I begged him to stop. Yesterday, he had revealed his weakest, most vulnerable side and now it was obvious to me that he was overcompensating, hoping that if he made me laugh I might forget what I had seen. But I couldn't forget. Images of his blood on the carpet kept flashing into my mind, each time jolting me with shock. I felt awkward around Danny, scared to say anything that might upset him and send him back over the edge again.

Mum had been ringing sporadically ever since I'd left home. She'd left pitiful-sounding messages on my voicemail, begging me to call her and sort things out. Guiltily, I had ignored all but the first, to which I'd sent a text in reply: DON'T WORRY ABOUT ME. I'LL CALL WHEN I'M READY.

That day, after what had happened with Danny, I felt differently. I actually wanted to see her. I needed a hug from somebody who could make me feel loved and protected. So when Danny was in the toilet, I texted her: CALL ME IF U WANT 2 TALK.

A few seconds later, my phone began to ring.

'Naomi, I'm so glad to hear from you,' Mum said breathlessly.

'You all right, Mum?'

'Yes, yes. And you?'

'I'm fine,' I lied.

'I'd really like to see you, Naomi. Would you think about coming home this afternoon? I promise you Dad's at work – it'll be just the two of us.'

I considered the offer. On the one hand, I welcomed the idea of some space from Danny so I could get my head straight, but on the other, I was frightened of how he would react and what he might do. I knew he saw my parents as a threat and I didn't want to risk angering him. And then there was the question of whether it was safe to leave him alone. Would he trust me not to reveal his secret? He had no cause to worry. Much as I needed to talk, I already knew I had no intention of betraying his confidence to Mum. I couldn't bear the thought of her pitying Danny or thinking of him as weak or ill.

'Hold on a sec, Mum,' I said. 'I'll ring you back.'

I knocked on the bathroom door. 'Danny – would you mind if I went out for a couple of hours? Mum's just called. I just want to keep the peace, you know?'

'Of course not,' he said, perhaps too brightly. 'I've had a great idea for a song. You go out and leave me to it.'

Allowing myself to be reassured, I called Mum back. 'OK,' I said. 'I'll come over. But just for an hour or so. I'm not staying.'

Mum was ever so formal when she opened the door to me – she greeted me almost like a stranger. Her jaw was clenched tight with nerves and her hands were sweaty and fidgety. *She's holding back because she's scared of me*, I thought, and I hated myself for it. The longed-for hug didn't materialise. I wanted to say, 'It's me, *Naomi*,' but I knew that if I let my guard down everything would all come pouring out. I had to stay strong, for Danny's sake.

When we were sitting together at the kitchen table Mum took a deep breath and began a conversation that she had evidently rehearsed several times in her head.

'I understand what you're going through – far more than you realise,' she began.

'What do you mean?' I asked nonchalantly. I sat stiffly, my arms folded on the table in front of me. My body language spoke volumes. 'Here we go,' it said. 'Another lecture.'

'Hear me out, Naomi. I understand, because I've been there myself. With someone a lot like Danny, actually. Before your dad.'

I studied her quizzically. As far as I was concerned,

Mum and Dad had been together since the year dot, since the Big Bang. I had never considered that Mum might have had a life – and relationships – before she met him.

'Yeah, right.' I managed a smirk. 'What, at nursery school?'

But she wasn't smiling. He expression was deadly serious.

'Stay there, Naomi,' she said. 'I'm just going to get something.'

She went upstairs and it sounded like she was moving furniture around. When she returned, looking flustered, she was carrying something in her hands. It was an old cardboard box. She rummaged around in it and pulled something out, which, after a moment's hesitation, she placed on the table in front of me.

'Look, Naomi.'

I looked. It was a photograph of two young people, their arms wrapped around each other. The image confused me. At first glance it appeared to be a picture of me, but I didn't recognise the guy or the hippie-style clothes I was wearing, and I knew I'd never grown my hair that long. It couldn't be me. And yet, something about the girl's smile was familiar.

I looked at Mum, then back at the photograph, and back at Mum again.

'It's you, isn't it?' I cried. I'd never seen Mum like this before – in all the photos she'd shown me she resembled a younger version of herself, with short, sensible, mousy hair, glasses and frumpy clothes. This was a period of her life I knew nothing about.

She laughed. 'Of course it's me. I wasn't born middle-aged, you know. Who else could it be?'

'Actually, you look like a lot like me,' I said. 'In horrible, polyester seventies' clothes. You look kind of cool, though,' Seeing her now, it was hard to believe that she had ever been young and pretty and – for the time – fashionable.

She laughed again. 'I guess I do. I was about your age there – a year or two older, perhaps.' Mum sighed. 'Hunky guy, isn't he? A bit of a dish?'

I hated it when Mum spoke like that; it was so embarrassing.

'He's not bad,' I conceded. 'If you take away the purple paisley flares. Nice eyes. Who is he?'

'His name was – and still is, I presume – Dominic Clearey, and,' she breathed deeply, 'he was the love of my life.'

I was shocked. 'What, more than Dad?'

'No, don't get me wrong, I love your Dad too. He's a wonderful man. But Dominic was my first love – my soul-mate, as you put it. He was "the one".'

'Why are you telling me this?'

'Because I love you,' she said. 'And I think you need to hear it. I've never told anyone this before – not even your dad knows the full story. Please hear me out.'

I nodded, still sceptical that anything she said would make a difference, but intrigued nonetheless.

And this, more or less, is the story she told me:

Once upon a time there was a young girl named Martha Brookes who had an enormous musical talent.

People came from far and wide to hear her play the piano and she was awarded with prizes and scholarships to the country's top music schools. It was generally agreed that one day she would make her name as a world-renowned pianist. She practised hard, passed all her exams with flying colours and, at eighteen, took her place at the Royal Academy of Music.

But Martha was a dreamer. She dreamed of love and of passion with dark strangers from faraway lands. She was tired of practising hard, of playing the same phrases over and over again until her fingers ached. She longed for escape and adventure.

One night, at a concert, Martha met a man named Dominic Clearey. Half Irish, half Indian, he was the exotic, dark-eyed knight of her dreams. He swept her off her feet and made her feel that she was beautiful and special. Nobody had ever complimented her on anything but her piano playing and for the first time, she felt alive.

Dominic introduced her to new types of music, which weren't played in stuffy concert halls, and he and took her to festivals all over the country in his camper van. The more time Martha spent with Dominic, the less she practised the piano. The accolades stopped coming and the invitations to give recitals dwindled, but Martha didn't care. All she wanted was to be with Dominic.

When Dominic asked Martha to move in with him she did so without a moment's thought. Her parents were horrified, but she ignored their advice. She dropped out of college, thinking that she could return in the future, when she was ready.

It soon transpired that Dominic was not the knight in shining armour she had imagined. He didn't want her to get a job, but criticised her housekeeping abilities, making her feel that nothing she did was good enough. He went out with his friends nearly every night, rolling in drunk in the early hours. And then, one night, he didn't come home at all. A few days later he rang Martha to tell her that he'd met somebody else, somebody more beautiful and more interesting. He told her to pack her things and to leave his house.

Martha was devastated. She returned home to her parents and began practising the piano again. But it was too late. There was no longer a scholarship or a place for her at the Royal Academy; younger and more prodigious talents had usurped her. So Martha put away her dreams of fame and of love, and trained as a teacher.

A few years later, she met David Waterman, the man who turned out to be her real white knight. He wasn't as passionate or exciting, but he was kind, hard-working and stable and all he wanted was to make Martha happy. Slowly, she let go of her feelings for Dominic and fell in love with David. Eventually, she married him, bore him two children and now, as everyone knows, they are living happily ever after.

When Mum had finished telling me her story she looked at the photograph again, smiled sadly, and then put it away in the box.

'Do you see, Naomi? Do you see?' she asked. 'I

thought Dominic was the only man for me, but in the end he didn't make me happy. If I hadn't met him I could have achieved so much more ...' She paused, sighing deeply. 'And, even if things with Dominic had worked out, then I wouldn't have met your dad and I'd never have had you and Emily.'

'I'm sorry about what happened to you, but what has this got to do with me and Danny?' I asked. I wasn't stupid; I knew exactly why she had told me her cautionary tale, and that she wanted me to understand that she had once been young and idealistic, just like me – but I wasn't ready to accept it. So I played dumb.

'Oh, Naomi, can't you see? I just don't want you to make the same mistakes I did.'

'I'm me,' I said. 'And Danny's Danny. He's not Dominic. Just because you had a bad experience doesn't mean I will. I love Danny and I know he loves me.'

I may have sounded confident, but it was just an act. Underneath, I was a quivering wreck, desperate to tell her how worried I was about Danny, that he hurt himself and that I didn't know how to help him. I wanted to admit that being with him was no picnic, and that she might even be right about him. But I couldn't. I'd promised to keep Danny's secret. How could I betray him now? How could I let him down when he needed me most? I needed to be strong, for both of us.

'I know what I'm doing, Mum,' I said. 'I'm old enough to live my own life.' I almost added, 'and make my own mistakes,' but I didn't want to contemplate that possibility.

'You're right,' said Mum. 'You're old enough to make your own decisions. But please think about what I've said. Take your time, but think about it.'

'All right,' I agreed. I owed her that, at least. 'I'll give you a call in a couple of days.'

Chapter 16

I thought about what Mum had told me all the way back to Danny's. Her account really did seem like a fable or a fairy tale to me – a story with a moral, about someone I had never known. It was ironic, really. I had gone home to see Mum because I needed security and familiarity, and instead, I had found out that there was so much about her that I didn't know, that I only knew a little bit of her. She had lived a whole, other life in which Dad, Emily and I had played no part. Mum looked the same, spoke in the same voice, smelled of the same rose-tinged perfume, yet she had somehow changed. It unnerved me to realise that even the people you are closest to have secrets – memories, thoughts and dreams that they keep locked away from the world. It made me wonder if it was ever possible to know anyone completely. Even Danny. Could there be more secrets to uncover? The idea made me shudder.

Thinking about Mum loving anyone other than Dad made me feel uncomfortable too, as though I was being unfaithful to him. How horrible for Dad, I thought, that much as Mum loved him, she could describe somebody else as 'the one', that he was, unwittingly, second best. It made me realise, however, that what I had with Danny was unique to us. Mum had made herself get over Dominic, but her feelings for him hadn't vanished, they were and always would be tucked away at the back of her mind. Soulmates don't come along very often – once in a lifetime, if you're lucky. And only one person can ever be your 'first love'. If, as my parents wanted, I left Danny, I might never find love like this again. Mum hadn't – she'd admitted as much.

Mum had told me about her past because she wanted me to finish with Danny. I'm sure she hadn't anticipated that her revelations might backfire on her. Yet, backfire they did. By the time I reached Danny's front door I had convinced myself that, whatever his problems, I wanted to be with him, to help him. Our love was strong enough to overcome anything, I told myself. This was a once-in-a-lifetime relationship and I had to give it my all. I was only eighteen, there was no way I was ready to give up on him – on love – and settle for second best.

Whenever I pictured Danny in my mind's eye I saw him as he was on stage, at my first Wonderfulls gig: tall and powerful and unfeasibly handsome. As I made my way back to his flat, I imagined that this was the Danny who would be waiting for me there. I would let myself in and then run straight into his arms, so I could tell him how much I loved him, how lucky I was to have him. Everything would be perfect again – of that I had no doubt.

But when I went into the living room and saw him – for real – all my hope and excitement drained away. He was lying on the sofa watching a kid's cartoon. He hadn't shaved or got dressed and his breakfast plate was still on the floor, where he'd left it. There was no sign that he'd done any songwriting; his guitar was in its case, leaning against the wall, just as it had been when I'd gone out. My pleasant fantasy melted into a pool of disappointment and, for a brief moment, I actually hated him.

'What have you been doing?' I asked, irritated.

'Oh, you know, this and that,' he said. He stretched out on the sofa. 'How was your mum?'

'She was good,' I snapped. I didn't want to talk about it. 'Are you going to get dressed today?'

He looked daggers at me. 'Where did that come from? Did your mum tell you to say that?'

I ignored him. 'It's after three, Danny. We could do something if you got dressed.'

'I don't feel like doing anything.'

'Maybe that's why you're so miserable. How can I help you if you won't let me?'

'I'm not miserable,' he barked. 'I'm perfectly happy sitting here. You're the one with the problem.'

'I'm going to lie down,' I said. I didn't want another argument. 'I'll see you later.'

I can honestly say that I have never been so confused in my life. My brain literally ached with it all. I absolutely, totally and utterly loved Danny. I loved his intelligence and his talent and his wit. I loved the way he looked. I loved talking to him, hearing him play and sing. I loved being in his arms, the way he made me feel. But maybe I wasn't in love with the real Danny. Maybe *this* was the real Danny: this lazy, depressive, aimless person, who hurt himself. Could I love this Danny? And if I couldn't, did that mean I didn't *really* love him after all? Did that make me selfish or shallow? Or was this just a phase, something that he would get over – something that I could help him through?

I needed somebody to talk to, somebody who could help and advise me. But who? Danny's mum plainly wasn't interested in her son and my parents had made their feelings clear. My friends weren't around (this wasn't something I wanted to talk about in a snatched phone conversation or by e-mail) and, anyway, I wasn't sure that Debbie, or anyone else, would understand. Emily wouldn't get it – she'd just think Danny was weird. As for Danny's friends, I didn't know any of them well enough to confide in. But even if there had been someone I could talk to, I had promised Danny that I wouldn't betray his confidence.

So there it was: I was utterly alone. There was only one person whom I felt was there for me completely, and that was Danny. But *he* was the problem. My brain whirred round and round and round, tangling my thoughts and feelings like a ball of wire wool, slicing deep into every nerve and every axon. Thinking was agonising, tortuous. Was this, I wondered, how Danny felt when he cut himself? I was beginning to see how physical pain might be preferable to mental torment. Perhaps it would work for me too. Perhaps if I experienced what he experienced everything would become clear.

I opened my overnight bag and took out my nail scissors, pulling them apart so that I could find the sharpest side.

Then, clenching my teeth, I held out my hand and ran the cold metal along my knuckles. I felt nothing but a sharp scratch; the scissors were too blunt to break the skin.

What are you doing, Naomi?

It was the first clear thought I'd had all day. I realised that my forehead was clammy and my limbs shaky – my body had begun to shut down, preparing itself for pain, for injury. I never had been able to deal with the sight of my own blood; if the scissors had done their nasty job I would have passed out. I took a deep breath. *Stupid, stupid girl.* Hurting myself wasn't going to help Danny and it certainly wouldn't help me. What I needed was space – time and space to think things through properly.

I went back downstairs. Danny was still sitting where I'd left him. He looked up at me, hopefully. 'Have you calmed down now?' he asked. 'Look, I'll get myself together and then we can go out somewhere, OK?'

'I don't think so, Danny,' I said. I swallowed hard, summoning my courage. I was aware that what I was about to say defied almost every instinct I possessed. 'I think I should go home, just for a week or so, to get my head sorted.'

He looked as if I'd kicked him in the stomach. 'What? You're leaving me?'

'No, just moving home for a bit. I still love you, Danny. But I'm so confused.'

'Love?' He pronounced it like the lash of a whip. 'You don't know the meaning of the word.'

If he had intended to inspire guilt, it worked. He couldn't possibly have known how much that comment

Loving Danny

hurt me. The only thing I did know, clearly and unquestionably, was that I loved him. 'Please understand. I just need some time.'

I walked over to him and put my arms around his neck. I thought he was going to cry, but then his face hardened.

'Just go, Naomi,' he said, pushing me away. 'Go now.'

Chapter 17

I had no contact with Danny for three long weeks. Which was, I calculated, a total of twenty one days; five hundred and four hours; thirty thousand, two hundred and forty minutes; or one million, eight hundred and fourteen thousand, four hundred seconds. I was painfully aware that each moment that passed was another moment without him. And yet, conversely, time also stood still. I barely noticed that the days slipped into weeks because I was at a standstill, living the same empty day again and again, endlessly thinking the same thoughts and feeling the same contradictory emotions.

Three weeks of thinking left me no less muddled, no closer to finding the answers I needed. And three weeks alone did nothing to dull my feelings for Danny or to dispel the sense that, without him, I was lost, incomplete. I didn't want to experience anything new if he couldn't share it with me. Hearing a funny joke or reading an interesting story no longer gave me pleasure, because Danny wasn't there to enjoy it too. I'd often catch myself thinking, *I must show Danny that,* or, *Danny would love this,* and then I'd feel bereft because I couldn't tell him about it. Being apart from Danny was like having an itch beneath my skin that couldn't be scratched.

He didn't ring me; I'd asked him not to. That didn't stop me checking my mobile several times a day, hoping at the very least for a missed call. Sometimes I wondered if he was not calling because he was trying to punish me or because he didn't want to talk to me. I'd told him I would call when I was ready, but when would that be? Many times I had to force myself not to pick up the phone and tell him what a huge mistake I'd made. But until I was sure what I wanted, what was the point?

I wondered how long he would wait for me and worried that while I tried to decide what I wanted, he might make a decision for me. Images of his letter on my doormat after our first argument haunted me. Would he send another – a more cruelly worded one that couldn't be disregarded? Every morning, when I went downstairs, I had to steel myself in case a white envelope had appeared unnoticed while I slept. I knew that, this time, telling him I loved him wouldn't be enough. He didn't believe it, because he thought I had left him.

I couldn't bear to think of the relationship being over – and even worse, if it were over, it would be my fault. Fear gnawed constantly at my ribs. Surely our last kiss hadn't been our final kiss? It hadn't seemed special or significant at the time – I wished it had been. I tried to recall its every detail, how it had felt, how Danny had tasted. But as the days went by, my memory dulled and it was harder and harder to relive it. Soon it was only a shadow of a kiss, no more real to me than looking at an old photograph of two lovers embracing.

Guilt kept me awake at night. Had I been selfish and cruel? Did Danny think I had abandoned him? Was he now hurting himself because of me? That was the thought that most scared me: Danny bleeding, in pain, perhaps cutting too deep this time, and nobody knowing. Would he call me if that happened?

In practical terms, my life resumed as before. Mr Stevens allowed me to return to the law firm, on the condition that I applied myself and took no more days off. Pleased to have something to fill my time, I did my job on autopilot, performing every task that was demanded of me with a forced smile, so that nobody could complain about my attitude or my mood. I varnished my new conscientious image by staying late on several occasions. The truth was, I wanted to delay going home to nothing, and to avoid the small chance of bumping into Danny on the high street.

Evenings and weekends were interminable. I read I don't know how many novels to try to take my mind off Danny, but I couldn't absorb myself in the characters' lives. Every mention of love, every disagreement, made my mind jump to thoughts of my own situation. It didn't matter whether the hero was named John or Cal or even Siegfried; to me, they were all called Danny, and the title of every book, *Loving Danny*.

My parents had initially been delighted when I came home. But seeing how miserable I was did not make them happy. I wouldn't – couldn't – talk to them about my feelings, so they gave up and left me alone, whispering about me when they thought I was out of earshot. Concerned that I wasn't eating properly, Mum went out of her way to make my favourite dinners. That only made me feel guilty too.

I don't think I could have survived those weeks without Emily. She did everything she could to take my mind off Danny, offering to take me shopping and inviting me out with her friends. Knowing what bad company I would be, I rarely accepted. It was nice to be asked, though. In return, I helped her with her coursework and lent her my clothes. She was welcome to them; I didn't feel like dressing up any more.

But sympathetic as she was, Emily didn't really understand what I was going through. To her mind, you were either happy or sad; you either loved someone or you didn't. Day after day, she begged me for an explanation, wearing me down with her anxious stares and generous hugs. And so, a week after I'd returned home, having sworn her to secrecy, I finally told her that Danny cut himself.

'Really?' she exclaimed, her eyes growing wide with surprise. 'There's a girl in my class who does that. She burns herself with cigarettes too. It's weird.'

'I know,' I said. After keeping the information to myself for so long, just saying it out loud was a tremendous relief. I was surprised at how little guilt I felt.

'God, Nay, I can't even wax my own legs or pull off a plaster myself, because I'm scared it will hurt.'

'Me neither,' I said, ashamed at the memory of my failed attempt to cut myself with scissors.

'How long has he been doing it for?'

'I don't know.' I felt foolish. Should I have realised what Danny's scars meant the very first time I saw them? Would anyone else have know right away?

'Wow,' exclaimed Emily, for want of something better to

say. But I could tell that a little part of her was impressed. Cutting himself gave Danny some sort of cachet – she thought it was a cool, dangerous rock-star thing to do.

I rolled my eyes at her to make it clear she was way off track.

'So what are you going to do?'

'I don't know,' I said.

She hugged me. She didn't have any answers – I hadn't expected that she would. 'I'm sure it'll be all right,' she said. 'You'll work it out.'

I wasn't sure whether 'it' referred to Danny's problem or to our relationship and, whatever she meant, I wasn't convinced that I believed her. But it was good to hear.

One evening, when my mood was at its lowest, Debbie rang. I was surprised at how pleased I was to hear from her. Since her visit we had continued to speak once a week or so – out of habit, I suppose – but our conversations had been awkward and unsatisfying. I had self-edited any information about Danny because I felt she would judge him, so we'd stuck to safe subjects: our families, films and TV programmes and general small talk. Now that Danny and I were apart, I was aware just how much I missed the closeness we'd shared before she went away.

'Hi, Naomi,' she said warmly. 'Are you OK?'

'Yes, thanks, I'm fine,' I lied. 'How are you?'

'You don't sound fine,' she said tentatively. 'Your voice is weird. I know it sounds silly, but I've been thinking about you all day and worrying, and I just felt I had to ring you.'

We'd had this kind of 'telepathic' connection in the past – it's not uncommon between best friends. Often, I would pick up the phone to dial her number and she would already be on the line, having dialled me simultaneously. Was it possible that we still had it, despite everything?

'That's nice of you,' I said. I wasn't sure how to broach the subject of Danny. 'I've been better.'

'Has something happened with Danny?' she asked.

I hesitated. 'We're going through a bit of a rough patch. We're having a sort of break.'

'Oh, Naomi,' she said, with genuine concern. 'I know how much you love him. It must be horrible.'

That was the cue I needed to let it all come flooding out: the self-harm, my parents, my confusion. It was the second time I had betrayed Danny's confidence, but yet again I felt no guilt, only release. Debbie listened patiently, saying nothing until I had finished.

'Oh, Naomi,' she said again. 'Is there anything I can do? Do you want me to come down?'

'Thanks but no, Deb. There's no point. I've got to get my head straight.'

'It's a lot for you to deal with,' she said. 'I wish I had some useful advice, but I haven't got a clue what to suggest. All I can say is that Danny doesn't know how lucky he is to have you. You're so strong and kind and patient – anyone else would have fallen apart completely. What's happened isn't your fault, you know? Give yourself time and then do whatever you think is best. But remember to look after yourself too.'

There was no criticism, no 'I told you so' or 'you'd be better off out of it'. It occurred to me how foolish I had been to keep my distance from Debbie. She wasn't the enemy after all.

'Thanks, Debs,' I said, my voice beginning to crack with emotion. 'That means a lot.'

'Promise you'll call if you need me,' she said. 'If you want to talk about this more, any time, I'll be here for you. Really.'

I wasn't sure if I would call her, but now, at least, I felt that I could.

'I promise.'

On a dreary Sunday afternoon, three weeks after I'd come home, I decided to give in to temptation and log on to The Wonderfulls' website. I had avoided it for as long as I could, aware that the sight of my pictures would bring back troublesome memories. But I was sick of treading water and getting no closer to an answer; I felt I needed a tangible reminder of Danny.

I typed in the address – www.thewonderfulls.co.uk – and took a deep breath as I waited for the home page to load. I wondered if anybody had updated the site since I'd last worked on it, whether there was any band news, or if new gig dates had been posted. I hoped not; that was my job – I wasn't quite ready to give it up.

But there was no home page. All the pictures, all the text, all the links had vanished. Instead, there were just three enormous words, filling the screen:

I MISS YOU

I blinked hard. Were my eyes playing tricks on me? Had I typed in the wrong address?

But there was no mistake. Danny had sent me a message. I had told him not to contact me, so he had used the only forum open to him – a public one – to let me know how he felt. He missed me and he didn't care who knew it.

My brain went into overdrive. How long had the words been up there? How many other people had seen them before me and wondered what they meant? Did Danny think I had ignored them? Had he taken my silence as my response? He didn't know that I hadn't looked at the site until that day. What must he now be thinking – that I didn't love him, that I didn't care?

But I did care. The absolute knowledge of this hit me

like a sledgehammer. I cared about him more than anything –
I was a fool not to have realised it. Being away from him
hadn't made me happy and it had solved nothing. So what if
he was difficult? So what if he had problems? So what if my
parents thought he was a bad influence? So what! If he
needed help, I would help him. I wanted to be with him
regardless. I could actually feel my love for him flooding
back into my body, surging through my veins, hammering
on my heart and making my lungs expand. After weeks of
vacillation, Danny's message had made my decision for me.
It wasn't rational – something inside me had just clicked into
place.

I was a bundle of energy and excitement, unable to sit
still for a moment longer. I got up from the desk and ran
into the hall, banging on Emily's door with my fist. I had
to show her the website and tell her that I had decided
to get back together with Danny. I wanted to ask her
advice on what to say to him and to discuss the best way to
tell our parents. 'Wake up, Em!' I shouted. She didn't
respond. I pushed the door. 'I'm coming in – I hope you're
decent.'

I hadn't seen her all morning. She had gone to a party
the night before – another invitation that I'd declined – and
she still hadn't surfaced. I found her lying in her bed, her
eyes half-open. She didn't smile when she saw me.

'Wake up, lazy bones,' I said, bouncing on her bed. 'I've
got something to show you.' I was so animated that I could
hardly contain myself. I was jumping up and down, like a
dog ready to play ball.

'Go away, Nay,' she growled. 'I want to go back to sleep.'

'It's the middle of the afternoon. Must have been some party.'

She pulled herself up, rubbing her eyes. 'It was OK.'

'You've got to come into my room – I want to show you something.'

She didn't move. I took her arm, literally dragging her out of bed and pulling her through the door, across the hall and into my room. 'Look!' I cried. 'Look at this!'

When she saw the computer screen, she froze. She shook my hand from her arm and she dropped her head, her eyes beginning to fill with tears. It was not the reaction I had anticipated.

'What's wrong, Em? Can't you see? It's great! He loves me so much that he's done this. Isn't it great?'

'No,' she sobbed. 'No.'

'Emily, what's the matter?'

She gulped. 'I've got something to tell you, Nay. You're not going to like it.'

Chapter 18

'**D**anny kissed me.'

Danny kissed me. It was the last thing I'd expected her to say, absolutely the worst thing she could have said. My brain shut down with shock. I understood the words, but I couldn't process them.

'What? When?' We were still standing in front of the computer, the words 'I MISS YOU' shouting from the screen, like a cruel joke.

'He kissed me. At the party last night. He was there with some friends – I think he knew someone's brother.'

'Danny kissed you?'

She nodded. 'I'm so sorry, Nay.'

I felt as if I had been lifted off the ground and turned inside out. I was aware that I was involuntarily holding my breath, that I had stopped blinking and swallowing. This couldn't be real – it was like finding myself in an episode of a bad soap opera. Emily was my sister. I loved her, trusted her, confided in her. She knew everything there was to know about Danny. How could this have happened? How could she have let it happen?

Then my brain conjured up an image of Danny, his arms around Emily's slim neck, and I wanted to vomit. She had been wearing my top; it had still smelled of my perfume.

'Did you kiss him back? Was it a full-on snog?' The shock was speaking for me. I don't know why I asked that question – I didn't really want to know the answer.

'Not really.' She hesitated. 'Just for a second . . . a tiny bit.'

I remembered again my last kiss with Danny – it was what I had been grasping on to, our final intimate moment before everything fell apart. Now Emily, my confidante, my only support, had stolen even that from me. It was tainted, defiled. I had nothing left of him.

My shock turned to anger. 'You bitch!' I spat. 'Did you enjoy it?'

'Stop it, please.' She was crying so much she could hardly breathe. 'I'm sorry, Nay, I'm sorry. I'm being totally honest with you here – I don't want to lie to you. But it all happened so quickly. I'd had too much to drink, I wasn't thinking—'

'Oh, stop blubbing.' I'd had no idea I could be so cold, but I couldn't stop, couldn't help myself. 'Did you flirt with him? Did you want to look cool in front of all your friends? Did you?'

'No, Nay, I swear. It wasn't like that. We were just talking – about you, actually – and he looked so sad and I gave him a hug, and it just happened. I didn't plan it, honest.'

I'd seen the way Emily had looked at Danny, the way her friends looked at him. I thought, *She must have loved the attention – a gorgeous, older guy, wanting to talk to her, to kiss her. She lapped it up, didn't she?*

I said, 'I don't believe you.' But even as I said it, I knew

I didn't really mean it. I was thinking more clearly now. Blaming Emily was so much easier than allowing myself to blame Danny, shouting at her far less scary than the prospect of confronting him.

'You've got it all wrong. I was telling him you still loved him and that I thought you should get back together. I told him I thought he was great for you and that you'd work it out.'

'And so he kissed you? It doesn't make sense.'

'I know,' she said. 'I know. But I stopped him straight away – I promise. I told him it was wrong and that it shouldn't have happened.'

'And what did he say?'

'I can't really remember. He said not to tell you. I went to the loo with Katy and when we came back he'd just gone.'

'How convenient.'

Then a thought struck me. 'Were you going to tell me about this? If I hadn't shown you the website, would you have told me?'

'I . . . don't . . . know,' she hiccoughed. 'I hadn't thought it through yet.'

'I wish you'd never told me,' I said, remembering how happy I had been just a few minutes earlier. Now everything was more messed up than ever.

'Really? You'd rather I'd lied?'

'No. No. I just wish none of it had happened. I can't deal with this, any of it.'

She tried to hug me, but I was still too angry with her. 'Leave me alone, Emily,' I said. 'I need to talk to Danny.'

'Please don't hate me, Nay,' she whispered as she left the room. 'Please.'

I don't hate you, I thought. But I was too pig-headed to say it.

I went straight round to Danny's, before I could change my mind or start to rationalise what Emily had told me. I wanted to surprise him, to hear what he had to say before he could invent an explanation. Most of all, I wanted to see him again. It's stupid, I know, but I had the feeling that, somehow, everything could still be all right, that this could all go away.

I let myself into his flat, leaving the door on the latch so he wouldn't be alerted to my arrival. Hearing music playing in the living room, I went into his bedroom and sat on his bed, knowing that he would come in eventually. I was annoyed that I hadn't thought to redo my make-up before I left the house – I didn't want Danny to know what a mess I was inside. It was written all over my face in tear-streaked mascara.

I didn't have to wait long before Danny sauntered in, humming to himself. My heart leapt – in spite of myself, I fancied him as much as ever. It took a moment before he saw me, and then he jumped back on himself, his mouth falling open with surprise.

'Omi! Oh my God! What are you doing here?'

'Hello, Danny.' I smiled. I felt strangely calm.

He looked at me, confused, unnerved. I knew he was wondering if I had come because of his message or because Emily had told me what happened. He was trying to work out why I had hidden myself in his room, rather than call or text him to say I wanted to see him. My smile revealed nothing.

'Omi, it's so good to see you,' he said, rushing over to me. 'I've missed you so much.' I felt the sensation of his mouth on mine and I couldn't help but kiss him back. It was familiar and comfortable and yet new and exciting, all at the same time. God, I had missed his kisses.

Don't forget why you're here, Naomi, I told myself.

I pulled away. 'Missed me? Not that much,' I said cryptically.

He knew, then, that I knew. His voice rose by an octave. 'What do you mean?'

'Why don't you tell me what happened at the party last night? Or should I call Emily and get her to come round here.'

'What's she been saying?'

'Don't play dumb. She told me what happened. She said you kissed her. Why did you do it, Danny?'

'You've got it wrong,' he said. 'She's lying.'

'She's my sister. Why would she say it if it wasn't true? She wouldn't lie to me.'

'No? Never? And I would?'

How would you prefer to die, Naomi, by hanging or the electric chair? It's weird how your brain summons up long-buried memories at times of crisis. It was a game I'd played as a child, with the little boy who lived next door: decide which was the worse of two evils.

I don't want to die at all.

But you have to, Naomi.

Who did I want to be the liar: my only sister or the love of my life?

I'll take the forfeit.

Danny was right – Emily had lied to me before. She had lied about borrowing clothes and make-up and whether she'd stolen chocolate from the newsagent. Could she be playing some kind of sick game to make me finish with Danny?

It didn't make sense. Emily had nothing to gain by telling me about Danny's kiss – and everything to lose. I'd seen how painful recounting the kiss had been for her, knew that she had squeezed out every last, honest detail. But if Emily wasn't lying, then Danny must be. Hard as it was to admit it, I had known it all along, hadn't I? Why couldn't he simply have confessed and told me how sorry he was? Was his pride more important to him than the risk of losing me?

Danny took my silence to be my answer. He turned his back on me and began pacing the room. 'I can't believe you don't trust me. After everything we've been through, you still don't trust me.'

'It's not as simple as that. I want to trust you, Danny, but I'm so confused.'

I caught up with him, positioning myself between his body and the wall so that he had nowhere to go, so that he had to look at me.

'It is simple,' he said, shoving me out of the way and turning sharply, so that he had his back to me once again.

'Either you love me or you don't. Either you believe me or you don't. Yeah?'

I said nothing. There was nothing left to say.

It was over.

Chapter 19

That should have been the end of the story. In many ways, I wish it were. But nothing was ever neat with Danny; there were never any clear beginnings, middles or ends.

Of course, I didn't have the benefit of hindsight then. I left Danny's, certain that our relationship was over. I was broken and empty and exhausted and shattered, and all the other adjectives that don't quite express the indescribable pain of leaving someone you love. Most of all, I was terribly, terribly sad. Despite everything that had happened, I still loved Danny and I didn't know how I would ever stop. I knew that all I had to do was to go back and tell him that I believed him, and he would take me in his arms and everything would be all right. He still wanted me and I still wanted him – the fact that we couldn't be together was illogical. But how could I be with someone whom I didn't trust, someone who had looked me in the eye and lied?

I didn't allow myself to think about his reasons, to wonder whether he hadn't been able to help himself because he was hurting so much, or because he was on autopilot to self-destruct. What was the point? It would only cause me more confusion, more pain and more guilt. If he had done it because he was ill, then I had deserted him when he needed me most – and what sort of a person did that make me?

Somehow, I knew instinctively that the only way I could survive was if I thought of the relationship as dead. And so, when I arrived home, I found myself carrying out my own little mourning ritual. I got out all my photos of Danny and, one by one, took a last look at each image before putting it away in my bedside drawer. I was saying goodbye to my memories, filing them away in the past. Danny posing on stage: gone. Danny pulling a silly face: gone. Danny, his arm protectively around my shoulder: gone. Funny how the colours already seemed less vivid, our smiles ghostly. I could barely remember how I had felt in each captured moment, couldn't recall what had been said in the instant before the shutter clicked shut and the flash exploded. Even the photos taken only a month before now appeared years old – a life-time away. There would be no more gigs, no more hugs, no more kisses; the realisation struck me like a hammer to the chest.

I took my favourite photo of Danny out of its frame and studied it. It felt as if his eyes were following my gaze, his unfathomable expression begging me to reconsider, to help him. 'Stop torturing me, Danny,' I said aloud, but my conscience refused to obey. I kissed his face, before putting the photo away with the others. Then I cried until there were no tears left in me.

Afterwards, I felt numb, empty inside. The fog of emotion had cleared and, at last, I was able to focus, to think logically. I decided to write a list of all the reasons I'd ended the relationship, to help convince myself that I'd done the right thing.

1. Danny lied to me. *Can I ever trust him again?*

2. Danny kissed my sister. *And then tried to blame her. Ditto.*

3. Danny cuts himself. *It scares me and, no matter how much I want to, I don't know how to help him. I'm not wise enough, or strong enough.*

4. Danny is lazy. *He's barely done a day's work since I met him and he can't even be bothered to rehearse.*

5. Danny bitches about my parents. *But I love them and it makes me feel bad.*

6. Danny makes me question what I want to do with my life. *He confuses me.*

7. Danny hates his mum and dad. *OK, they're not the best parents, but I don't know if they've done anything to merit such vicious rage. It makes me uncomfortable.*

8. Danny is moody. *It puts me on edge.*

9. I never know quite where I am with Danny. *Ditto.*

10. Danny turns everything into a drama. *It's exhausting.*

11. My parents don't think I should be with Danny. *I'm sick of fighting with them.*

12. I'm supposed to be going away to university in

the autumn. *If I stay with Danny, I won't want to go.*

I couldn't think of any more. It was enough, wasn't it?

Then, almost inevitably, I suppose, I found myself composing a list of what was good about Danny.

1. I love Danny and he loves me. *There's no better feeling in the world, is there?*
2. Danny is my soulmate. *I might never find another.*
3. Danny is gorgeous. *Just looking at him gives me butterflies.*
4. Danny is spontaneous. *Being with him is unpredictable and exciting.*
5. Danny is clever and interesting. *I've learned so much from him. He's so stimulating.*
6. Danny makes *me* feel clever and interesting. Nobody else has ever done that.
7. Danny a) writes amazing songs and b) has an incredible voice. *He's so talented – he could be really successful one day.*
8. Danny is generous and thoughtful. *He's given me the most amazing presents.*
9. Danny makes me laugh. *He even laughs at my jokes.*
10. Kissing Danny.

I read through my lists several times. I had to acknowledge that there were more points in the negative list than in the positive, and that, collectively, the negative points out-weighed the positive. However much I enjoyed kissing Danny, loved hearing him play, laughed at his jokes, these things couldn't make up for his problems, his lie. It had come down to a simple mathematical calculation: I couldn't be with Danny because there were too many obstacles in our way. Following my heart had got me nowhere, so perhaps it was now time to follow my head.

Finally, I decided to write Danny a goodbye letter. I can't remember the exact words I used – I don't have a copy – but it was four pages long and detailed all the points in both my lists. I didn't know if I was doing the right thing, or how he would react, but I had to be honest, to articulate everything I had been unable to say before. It wasn't fair not to tell him the truth, was it? So I told him that I loved him, and that I would always love him, but I couldn't be with him. Maybe, one day, when I had finished university and he had sorted out his problems, we might try again. I wanted to say, 'Please wait for me, Danny,' but I knew it wouldn't be fair to ask that of him. I signed it, *Forever, Omi.*

As I sealed the envelope, I imagined the look on Danny's face when he read my letter and remembered how desperate I had felt when I'd received his. I wished that I could be there to hold him and wipe away his tears – the possibility that he might have another – more violent – reaction was too horrible to contemplate. I prayed he wouldn't hate me; I couldn't bear that.

I posted the letter in the postbox at the end of my street, waiting until I had heard it flutter down and hit the bottom before I turned and walked away. Now it was too late to change my mind. Danny's fate lay in the hands of a faceless postal worker.

I didn't tell my parents it was over with Danny until the next day. Mum said she would be there for me if I wanted to talk and reassured me that the pain I felt would fade. Dad just patted me on the back and told me I was being very mature. 'One day,' he said, 'you'll look back on this relationship and wonder what you ever saw in Danny.'

His blasé attitude irritated me. I wanted to ask him how he could be so sure. He had never known, and would never know, what it was like to have a soulmate, to share that once-in-a-lifetime connection that is beyond words.

I told Emily that I believed her and had forgiven her for the kiss, but try as I might, I couldn't remove the image of her with Danny from my mind. It was there when we chatted, when we hugged, when we laughed. Something fundamental in our relationship had shifted; it would take many months to repair it.

And so, I got on with the business of living without Danny. I kept myself as occupied as possible, working late and taking books and papers home to read. I e-mailed my friends abroad and rang Debbie for a long heart-to-heart. Aching for company and consolation, I told her I'd like to come up and stay with her for the weekend. I got back in touch with Dee and planned a summer holiday with her, after her A-level retakes. I even enrolled in an evening class in photography.

Of course I couldn't erase Danny from my mind

entirely. Everything reminded me of him: bus journeys, music, TV programmes, other couples holding hands. They taunted me, forcing me to recall what I had once enjoyed and to acknowledge what I had now lost. Crying became as natural to me as eating or sleeping – I couldn't remember a time when my eyes hadn't been sore and puffy. But I discovered that I was far stronger than I had realised. I didn't break. Whenever I felt upset I would look to the future for comfort – to new adventures at university, new places and new friends. Life would go on without him, propelling me forwards. Grateful as I was, it was depressing to accept that the future was unstoppable. As far as the universe was concerned, Danny and I were just specks of matter, tiny and insignificant.

And then Danny had to go and spoil it all with one last, dramatic performance. How could I have forgotten that he never left the stage without playing an encore?

Chapter 20

The call came at two p.m. on a Saturday afternoon, not quite two weeks since I'd last seen Danny. He hadn't replied to my letter and I had finally stopped expecting to hear from him. I no longer jumped each time my phone rang.

But, for a split second before my mobile began to vibrate, I saw a clear image of Danny in my mind, and I *knew* something was very wrong.

The number was unfamiliar.

'Naomi, it's Mike – you know, the keyboard player from The Wonderfulls.'

Why was Mike ringing me? How had he got my number?

'Mike? Hi, how are you?'

'Yeah, all right.'

I could tell from his anxious tone that he wasn't calling to make small talk. 'Listen, Naomi, I'm sorry, but I've got some really bad news.' He took a deep breath. 'Maybe you should be sitting down, or something. Danny's in hospital.'

'Oh God,' I said. I felt my legs buckle. 'Oh God.'

'He's at St Hilda's. I thought you'd want to know.'

My mouth was suddenly so dry that I could hardly speak. Had there been an accident? Was Danny ill? Had he hurt himself? 'What's happened? Is he OK?'

Mike took a deep breath. 'He took an overdose, Naomi. And he's cut himself up pretty bad. But he's OK. I'm going to see him this afternoon and I know he wants to see you. Would you like a lift?'

'Yes, please. I'd really appreciate that.'

I felt completely numb after our conversation, as if, subconsciously, I had been expecting this news. I was neither scared nor anxious – I wasn't aware of any emotion, or any sensation at all. And then, the strangest thing happened. It must have been the shock, but all I could think about was what to take Danny in hospital. What do you give somebody who's taken an overdose? Grapes? Chocolates? Magazines? Who could I ask? Danny had felt so desperate that he wanted to die – almost certainly because of me – and all I could worry about was whether to run to the corner shop and buy a pound of red seedless or the *NME*. I was driving myself mad with the simplest, most inane decision.

Mike rang the doorbell an hour later. I waited until he was standing on the doorstep before I told my parents where I was going, so they wouldn't try to stop me. I knew they'd never argue with me in public, in front of a stranger.

'Oh, Naomi,' said Mum sadly as I left. 'I do hope you know what you're doing.' Then, as an afterthought, 'Give Danny our best.'

The car journey was uncomfortable. Here we were, two people who hardly knew each other, thrown together by something unspeakably horrible. I wondered if Mike knew that Danny and I had split up and, if he did, whether he blamed me. Was it my fault? Had Danny hurt himself because I'd left him, because I sent that letter? *What have you done, Naomi, what have you done?*

'Have you brought him anything?' I asked. Anything to break the silence, to stop the guilty voices in my head.

'No,' he replied, glancing over at me. 'But I took him his iPod this morning.'

'You've already seen him?'

'I was the one who found him, Naomi – last night. I didn't want to call you until I knew he was all right. And it took some time to get your number.'

'You found him?'

'Yes. He called me yesterday afternoon, saying he wanted to rehearse. I thought it was odd; we never rehearse on a Friday and we haven't got together for weeks. I was the first to arrive. The door was on the latch and I found him lying semi-conscious on the living room floor and called an ambulance.'

'How awful,' I said, remembering the shock of Danny's blood on the carpet. Poor Mike. This must have been far worse.

He nodded. 'It wasn't nice.' He paused, evidently visualising what he had seen. 'He must have meant for me to find him. He'd taken some pills and cut a kind of circle into his arm, with a knife.'

'He cuts himself, Mike. He's done it before. Did you know that?'

He didn't flinch. 'Everyone knows Danny has problems. They've got worse since we didn't get the record deal.

To be honest, it's caused the band a lot of hassle. We were talking about winding it up.'

'Winding up The Wonderfulls? Oh my God. But you're so good.'

He smiled and shrugged his shoulders. 'Cheers for that. It's all getting to be too much like hard work, though.'

'Do you think it's my fault, Mike?'

'No!' He laughed. 'Of course not. You're the best thing that ever happened to him.'

He had meant to be kind, but hearing that made me feel even more guilty.

'I dumped him, Mike. A couple of weeks ago.'

'Oh, Naomi, he didn't tell me – I had no idea. I wouldn't have called if I'd known. He asked for you – I assumed you were still together.'

Danny hadn't told his friends we'd split up? Hadn't he understood my letter? How could he not believe it was over?

'No, no,' I said, shaking my head. 'I'm pleased you did. I still love him. I'd hate to think of anything happening to him and nobody telling me.'

We had arrived at the hospital. Mike parked and came round to my side of the car to open the door for me. *He's a gentleman*, I thought, *just like Danny*. We walked into the building together in silence and Mike called the lift. 'He's in a ward on the third floor,' he said, squeezing my shoulder. He had noticed that I was starting to shake. 'Let me go in for a couple of minutes first and then I'll come out and get you.'

I paced the corridor. St Hilda's is an old Victorian hospital,

Gothic and grand on the outside and dilapidated on the inside. The walls were yellow-white, the curtains faded and tatty, and the fixtures and fittings chipped and outdated. Thankfully, there was no smell. That's what I dreaded most about hospitals – the stench of urine and chlorine and sick all mixed together like the devil's perfume. My grandma had reeked of it when I went to visit her, a couple of years before. She had died the next day. Now, whenever I thought of her, I caught a whiff of it in my nostrils again. I didn't ever want to associate that smell with Danny.

Mike came to find me a few minutes later. 'He's OK,' he said. 'He's looking forward to seeing you. I'm going to get off now.' He kissed me on the cheek. 'Good luck.'

He pressed a piece of paper into my hand. 'My number – in case you need to call me.'

So Mike had only come back to bring me? What a kind thing to do. Perhaps, if things had turned out differently, we could have become friends. Now, I would probably never see him again.

I steeled myself before I pushed open the double doors and walked into the ward. *Daisy Ward*, it was called. *Danny would hate that*, I thought. It wasn't exactly rock and roll. I had no idea what to expect, what state Danny would be in, what he would look like.

A nurse stopped me. 'I'm here to see Danny Evans,' I said.

She smiled kindly. 'You must be Naomi. He's at the far end.'

I walked past rows and rows of beds: old men, dozing or

coughing; middle-aged men hooked up to machines and drips; young men staring vacantly into space. Some looked up at me expectantly, perhaps hoping that I might have come to visit them. It wasn't until I had neared the end of the room that I saw Danny. My stomach lurched. He was propped up against some pillows, wearing a blue hospital gown, with tubes coming out of his hand. His hair was lank and greasy and he had at least three days' growth on his chin. He didn't look like Danny – this guy was much older, much smaller in build. If I hadn't known he was there, I might have walked straight past him.

'Omi,' he croaked as I approached his bed. 'It's so good to see you. Thanks for coming – I knew you would.'

Did he?

He beckoned me to sit down beside him, moving his tubes out of the way. Now I could see that his arm was covered in a large dressing and there were black marks on his chin, remnants of the charcoal the doctors used to pump his stomach. He held out his hand and I took it. It was like holding hands with a ghost.

'Sorry about the wires,' he said. 'They've got me on an antibiotic drip, to stop infection.'

'Oh, Danny, what have you done? I've been so worried about you.'

'I'm sorry, Omi,' he said flatly. 'You shouldn't worry.' Then his voice became more animated. 'Look – I've got something to show you.' He dropped my hand and started to unwrap the dressing on his arm, wincing with pain as he did so.

'Don't,' I said. 'Please don't.'

But he ignored me. He pulled away the bandages and pointed to his arm. 'See it, Omi? See it?' I forced myself to look. There before me, on his forearm, was a large, deep, angry wound, in the shape of a uneven circle, just as Mike had described.

And then it hit me. It wasn't a circle. It was an O – O for Omi.

'I did it for you,' he said, almost proudly.

It was too, too horrible. I felt a rushing in my ears and, for a second, everything went black. I gripped the sides of the bed and breathed deeply, until the room came back into focus. How could I not have realised how ill Danny was? He was out of his mind. Even now, he was playing games with me. Just as he had planned for Mike to find him, so he had known that if he did something desperate I would come running back to him.

I couldn't look at him. 'No, Danny, no. This wasn't what I wanted. Don't you understand? It's not that I don't love you, it's just so difficult for me. And doing this doesn't help – it makes it worse.'

'I wanted to show you how sorry I was, how much I love you,' he pleaded. He tried to re-dress his arm, folding the bandage back over itself. But the ends hung limply, rolling outwards again and exposing his wound to the air.

'I'll get the nurse,' I said.

'No, stay and talk to me for a bit first please.'

'OK.' I took his hand again. I didn't know what to say.

'You could have just got a tattoo, like anyone else

would,' I said eventually. It was a feeble attempt at black humour.

He laughed, in spite of himself. 'That's what I love about you, Omi. You always speak your mind. Everybody else has been fussing around me, scared to say the wrong thing. How could I have let you go?'

'You kissed my sister,' I said, my voice suddenly serious.

He hung his head. 'I know and I'm so, so sorry. I'm sorry I did it and I'm sorry I lied. But I did it because I love you. I was missing you so much and then I saw Emily at the party and she reminded me of you and . . . it just happened. It was you I wanted, not her.'

It was an explanation, an apology, of sorts. *Too little, too late.*

'OK, Danny, I understand – kind of,' I said. 'But if you'd just come clean when I came round, we could have sorted it all out then. Maybe.'

'Don't you think I know that?' he said angrily. 'It wasn't till I got your letter that I realised what I'd done, and then it was too late.' His voice softened. 'All I've thought about for the past couple of weeks is you. You are the most important thing in my life, Omi. I don't care about my music, The Wonderfulls; none of it matters without you. Please give me another chance to prove it to you.'

He was so earnest, so desperate, that I felt my resolve beginning to slip. Maybe it was possible to make this work. Nobody would ever love me this much again, would they? Or was everything he was saying merely part of his illness?

'But you need help, Danny,' I said. 'You're not well.'

'I know,' he said, quietly. I could tell that it was a big deal for him to admit it. 'But if you're with me I can get better. You can help me get better. I'll stop cutting myself, I'll make us both happy. I need you, Omi – please help me.'

My head was spinning, my mouth parched. I got up from the bed. 'I need some air,' I said. 'I need to think. Give me ten minutes or so and I'll come back and see you. I will.'

He grasped my arm. 'OK,' he said, his eyes piercing into mine, as though he thought that if he tried hard enough he might be able to decipher my thoughts. 'Promise me.'

I didn't bother to wait for the lift. I ran down all three flights of stairs as fast as I could, unconsciously holding my breath until I reached the bottom. It wasn't until I had pushed through the hospital's front entrance doors that I stopped and leaned against the railings, gasping for air.

'Naomi?'

I looked up. It was Mrs Evans. She stood in front of me, dressed as immaculately as ever, in a slate grey suit and black stilettos. She was done up for a business meeting, not a hospital.

'Mrs Evans? Have you come to see Danny?' It was a stupid question, but as I've said before, she made me nervous.

'Yes,' she said, with a trace of sarcasm. 'Have you been in to see him already?'

'Just now,' I said. 'He's in a bad way – he showed me what he did. It was horrible. I think it's all my fault.'

'I doubt that very much, Naomi.' It was said not with kindness, but to make me feel that I was an irrelevance. 'It's not the first time this has happened and I dare say it won't be the last. Danny is a very troubled young man. He has been for several years.'

I was confused. 'What do you mean?'

'Come on, you're not telling me you thought you were dating Jiminy Cricket? Danny may be very intelligent and talented, but he's also oversensitive and his ego gets the better of him. He has a self-destructive side.'

She hadn't answered my question. 'What do you mean, it's not the first time this has happened?'

'He started cutting himself when he was thirteen – though, I grant you, he's not hurt himself as badly before. You must have seen the scars.'

I nodded. 'But the pills?'

'He tried that once before too, when he was fifteen. He didn't take enough pills to do much damage – then or now. He did it for attention, Naomi. Everything Danny does is for attention. When things don't go his way, he can't deal with it. It's always been the same. When he was ten, at his sister's eighteenth birthday party, he deliberately slammed the door on his hand because he felt left out and wanted everyone to focus on him.'

Sister? Danny didn't have a sister. He'd told me he was an only child. Was it another lie?

'His sister?'

'Stepsister,' said Mrs Evans. 'Danny didn't mention Sally? From my husband John's first marriage. She lives in America now.'

'Oh.'

'You're not the first girl to get sucked in by him. Lucy,

the girlfriend he went travelling with, she couldn't deal with it either. She left him in Colombo.'

I'd assumed that Danny had gone travelling with friends, not a girlfriend. He'd told me I was the only girl he'd ever loved. Had he told Lucy the same thing? Imagining Danny with anybody else made me feel sick to my stomach.

'I have no doubt he truly believes he loves you,' said Mrs Evans, as if she were reading my mind. 'But he'll use you as a crutch and eventually drag you down with him. Has he asked for your help, told you that you can save him?'

I nodded. *How did she know?*

She smirked. 'You can't help him, dear – he needs professional help. I should tell you that John and I have decided to pay for him to go into a private clinic, so he can get full-time care and intensive counselling. I tried once before – that's probably why he dislikes me so much. This time we won't take no for an answer. He won't get very far if we take away his trust fund, will he?'

'Oh,' I stuttered. 'No.'

It was all too much to take in. The sister, the ex-girlfriend, the trust fund: three fundamental aspects of Danny's life that I had known nothing about. Now I understood where he had acquired the money to pay for my gifts, for our expensive meals out. He didn't hate his car or his house, he hated himself for accepting them. He hated his parents because, without them, he would have had nothing.

Were omissions the same as lies? Danny may not have volunteered this information, but I had never asked. Had I been too scared of the answers to ask the right questions? Or was it his reaction that I'd feared?

Mrs Evans was suffocating me; I wanted her to leave me alone. 'You should go up and see him,' I suggested. 'I'm going to sit out here for a while and then I'll go back to the ward.'

She smiled, slyly, and proffered her hand. 'Goodbye, Naomi.'

I ignored her gesture. I no longer cared what she thought of me. She was a hateful, bitter woman – no wonder Danny was so messed up.

'Goodbye,' I said. *And good riddance.*

When she had gone, I found a bench in the hospital grounds and sat myself down, pushing my fingers in between the slats. The world was topsy-turvy and back to front. It even smelled different, the atmosphere heavier and darker, as if it had been laced with tar. Somehow, I had found myself in a parallel universe where Danny was a sick and needy stranger. However much I wished it wasn't true, *this* was the real world after all. The strong, confident Danny – the guy I had fallen in love with – had been an illusion; he had never existed.

Spiteful as she was, Mrs Evans was right about one thing: I couldn't help Danny. I wanted to, but what could I do? I wasn't a doctor or a counsellor, and I didn't want to be. Danny had been ill for years – what if he never got better? I was going to go to university, to become a lawyer or a photographer, or whatever I decided, one day. I didn't want to spend my life in dingy pubs, applauding Danny, soothing his ego when things didn't go well, putting antiseptic on his cuts. If I stayed with him, that might be my reality. And then it struck me: I didn't want to be his muse, I wanted to be *someone* myself, and I wanted a partner who could support me and be strong for me too. Danny needed time alone, to figure out who he was.

If Danny doesn't know who he is, how can he be my soulmate?

And if he is my soulmate, doesn't that make me as damaged as him?

Sometimes, the more you think, the less you understand. My mind was plagued by interference, like a radio caught between stations. I wished I could shut it up, switch it off.

I waited until I saw Mrs Evans leave the hospital and then I took the lift back up to the third floor. As the doors opened, I noticed that a slender girl was standing by the ward doors, with her back to me. There was something familiar about her posture, her colouring.

'Debbie?'

She turned round, startled. 'Naomi! Your parents told me you'd be here. I was starting to worry that I'd missed you.'

'I was just outside, having a think.' It was so good to see her. 'Oh my God, what are you doing here?'

She hugged me, tightly, and the warmth and familiarity of her embrace made my eyes begin to brim with tears. 'Your mum called me and told me what had happened. I was in the town centre already, so I just got straight on the next London train. I thought I should come down to be with you.'

I blinked hard. If I let myself begin to cry now, I might never stop. 'You came all the way down from Manchester just to see me?'

'Of course I did. You'd do the same for me, wouldn't you?'

'Yes, definitely,' I said, pleased that she'd want me to. Not that I could imagine that Debbie would ever find herself in a situation like this. 'Oh, Debbie, things are such a mess.'

'Do you want to go somewhere to talk?' she asked.

'Yes, please. Just give me a second – I need to say goodbye to Danny first.'

'Do you want me to come with you?'

I pondered her offer. While I welcomed her support, this was hardly the time to introduce the two of them. I didn't want to upset Danny, or embarrass him.

'No, I'll go in by myself, if you don't mind waiting.'

She hugged me again. 'Of course not.'

Danny was sitting up in bed, a half-read magazine lying open across his lap.

'You've been ages, Omi,' he said impatiently. 'I thought you weren't coming back.'

'I promised I would, didn't I?'

'I know, but you were so long that I was starting to get paranoid.' He laughed at his choice of word. 'Then again, I guess I'm entitled to be, considering everyone here thinks I'm a mental patient.'

He noticed that I wasn't smiling and his bravado

vanished. 'I wish you hadn't gone,' he continued. 'My mum was here – I told the nurse I didn't want to see her.'

I decided it was best not to mention my encounter with his mother.

'Don't be paranoid, Danny,' I said gently. It was best to come straight out with it. 'But I can't stay. Debbie's turned up. I need to spend some time with her.'

'Debbie?' He looked bemused. 'What's she doing here?'

'She came down to look after me.'

'Oh, I see.' But it was obvious that he didn't. The thought that I might need looking after because of what he had done was incomprehensible to Danny. I could tell he was thinking, *Hey, I'm the victim here.* He truly had no idea how much his actions had hurt me, how much I was hurting now.

'I was hoping we could spend some time together, talk about things,' he said. He looked so pitiful that for a moment I just wanted to forget about Debbie and hold him.

I steeled myself. 'We can. Just not today. I'm sorry.'

'Oh, OK.' There was desperation in his voice; he feared he was losing me. 'I was thinking – when I'm better I want to teach you how to play the guitar properly. And maybe we could go travelling together.'

'That would be nice, Danny.' I didn't mean to patronise him, but I couldn't deal with any more confusion – I had to get out of there. I kissed him lightly on his cheek. 'We'll talk about it tomorrow.'

'OK.'

As I turned away, he sank down in the bed and pulled

the covers over his head. I can't be certain, but I think he was about to cry. He didn't want me to see, and I didn't want to witness it.

Debbie stayed the night. We locked ourselves away in my room and talked for hours, just as we had always done before she went to Manchester. There was so much to tell her, all the anecdotes and details that I had missed out before, the things that would help her to understand why it was so hard to let Danny go. I took out my pictures, the notes, the song and the gifts he had given me, and we studied them in detail, as if we were collecting evidence for an autopsy of my relationship.

Some of what I related to her – such as our first date, the picnic – seemed to have occurred so long ago that it was like talking about another couple. It made me sad to realise that my memories and feelings were now coloured by what had happened later and by what I had learned about Danny. Why couldn't I have read between the lines of his lyrics and seen the anguish behind them? Had he really thought me special at all, or had he just seen in me a need to be wanted? I wept, often – tears of grief for what I had lost and for what might never have been.

Later, I made up a bed for Debbie on the floor next to mine and we carried on our conversation in the dark. It was easier to be candid when we couldn't see each other's faces.

She asked: 'How do you feel about Danny, Naomi?'

'You know how I feel – I love him.'

'That's too easy. I mean how do you really feel about

him – *now*? After everything? Do you still feel the same way you did? Honestly?'

'I don't know,' I said. 'When I looked at him in his hospital bed, he seemed so small and weak, so needy. I felt like I wanted to protect him and look after him.'

'Do you still fancy him?'

'Yes, of course. He's still gorgeous. But nobody's sexy when they're in hospital, are they?' As I said it, I realised that part of Danny's allure had been his strength, his mystery. Was he as attractive without them? I couldn't say it out loud, but I had to acknowledge that he wasn't.

Debbie hesitated. 'Don't take this the wrong way, but that makes it sound like you want to be his mother.'

I bristled. 'No, not exactly. If you love someone, you want to be there for them.'

'Sure,' she said. 'But what's in it for you?'

'I get to be with him. And perhaps . . . I don't know, when he's better maybe everything might be great again.' I pictured myself with Danny – saw us smiling and laughing – and, once more, my eyes brimmed with tears at the memory of what we had shared.

'You don't know that, Naomi. Will you really just be able to forget everything that's happened? And what if he doesn't get better? How long will you give it before you finally give up on him? A few months? A few years?'

'I don't know,' I sobbed. 'I haven't thought about it. Right now, I just want to help him. Just help him, you know?'

'Oh, Naomi,' she said, in her sweetest voice. 'Please

don't be upset again. It's not your fault. You can't make him better – he's the only one who can do that.'

'I know,' I croaked. I was gulping back the tears now, breathing too fast, my head growing light.

'Shh,' she cooed. 'Shh. It's all right, honey. It's going to be all right.' I sensed that she was moving and heard the rustle of her duvet. 'Budge up,' she said. She climbed into my bed and snuggled up to me, stroking my hair and smoothing the tear-dampened strands away from my face. Feeling her warm body against mine was such a comfort; for the first time in many weeks I didn't feel alone. We lay there, silently, until my sobs had subsided.

'I wish you weren't away in Manchester,' I said.

'I know. But I'm still here for you.'

'Thanks,' I said. 'That means a lot.' It meant the world to me. I felt that we had reached an understanding. Even if we couldn't share experiences first-hand we could still support each other. And, at last, I knew that despite our differences, our friendship could move forward.

'I think I pushed you away, Deb,' I said. 'I didn't intend to.'

'It's OK. It's my fault too. I was so caught up with uni and you were so caught up with Danny. It happens.'

'I'm not sure I can cope without him,' I said. 'I'm scared, Deb.'

'I know you'll be OK, whatever happens. Don't forget that you'd finished with him – you were getting on with your life. You were making plans. You're tougher than you think.'

'I wasn't happy, though. It felt like a big part of me was missing. I think I knew, deep down, that it wasn't really over – that something else would happen.'

Debbie was quiet for a moment. 'You know that John Donne poem about the compass, the one we did at school? Maybe that's how you should think of things with Danny. Maybe you have to let him go. If you really are soulmates, if you're really meant to be together, then, somehow, you'll find your way back to each other.'

Long after Debbie had fallen asleep, I lay awake, thinking about what she had said. Perhaps she was right. Perhaps the only way I would ever find out whether Danny and I were meant to be together was if we were apart.

> *If they be two, they are two so*
> *As stiff twin compasses are two;*
> *Thy soul, the fixed foot, makes no show*
> *To move, but doth, if th' other do.*
>
> *And though it in the centre sit,*
> *Yet when the other far doth roam,*
> *It leans and hearkens after it . . .*

By the time I waved Debbie off at the railway station, the following morning, I had made my decision.

Chapter 21

Isn't it weird how the truly significant days of your life often begin as the most banal? Isn't it? Debbie took the train back to Manchester, Emily got on with her homework and my mother cooked Sunday lunch. My bus took its usual route to the hospital, the traffic was as busy as ever, the other passengers as impatient and uncommunicative. Nobody asked me how I was or where I was going. And no one took any notice of the small rucksack I carried on my shoulder. The sky didn't fall in and the world kept turning.

The nurse grinned at me as I came into the ward. 'Hi, Naomi. I just need to let you know that we're moving Danny today, to the psychiatric unit.'

'That's OK,' I said. 'I'm only popping in for a minute.'

Danny's eyes lit up when he saw me. I noticed that he had washed and shaved and combed his hair, in preparation for my visit. He resembled the old Danny again, and it made my heart skip a beat. I had been a fool to think this would be easy, to believe I could control my emotions.

I swallowed. 'How are you?' I asked. 'You look better.'

He nodded and smiled and I looked at him, as if for the first time, taking in his beautiful eyes and the curve of his nose, trying to memorise the detail of his features and the way that he moved.

And then I kissed him. It wasn't a passionate kiss – the setting and the situation didn't allow for that – but it was a deep, slow, satisfying kiss that embodied all the emotions I felt but couldn't explain: hurt and regret, sorrow and fear, love and affection, loss and hope – all rolled into one wordless expression. I didn't want it to end.

Danny was the first to pull away. 'You're saying goodbye, aren't you?' he asked, his voice no more than a whisper. He looked into my eyes with a gaze so intense that I knew he had read my mind, that our connection remained as strong as ever. It was agonising. I had promised myself that I wouldn't cry again, but my tear ducts refused to obey. Salty water cascaded down my nose, into my mouth and my hair.

'I'm so, so sorry, Danny,' I said, forgetting the long speech that I had prepared. Quoting words from a poem seemed trite, telling him that he was in the best place, that I wasn't qualified to help him, patronising. Nothing I'd meant to say seemed relevant or important now. All I could muster was, 'I can't do this any more.'

I don't know whether it was arrogance or delusion, but he would not accept it. 'You're seriously giving up on us?' he asked, with a strange, guttural laugh that unnerved me.

'Yes, Danny,' I said. But I wasn't 'giving up' – that made it sound so easy. I was fighting every instinct and feeling that I possessed, trying to do what I thought was right.

'What – that's it? *Finito*? You're going to walk out on me when I'm in hospital?'

He was playing the guilt card. Of course he was – I should have anticipated it.

Be brave, Naomi, I told myself. *You're not a bad person. You're doing the right thing.*

'Yes, Danny, I'm sorry.' I couldn't look at him – it hurt too much. I wanted this to be over now. Clumsily, I unzipped the rucksack that I had brought with me. It contained some CDs, books and a sweater he'd lent me. 'Look, I've brought your things.'

'I don't want them,' he said, turning his head away. 'Hang on to them until I'm out of here and then we can talk about it.'

'No,' I said. 'There won't be another time. It's over.'

'You're kidding yourself, Omi. What we've got is too important for you to just walk away. You need me.'

He still didn't get it. Why didn't he get it? Was I going to be there all day, going round and round in circles, until I couldn't bear it any more and gave in? Why wouldn't he let me go?

'But I don't really love you any more,' I said. I hadn't intended to say it – at least I wasn't aware of any conscious thought process – the words just tumbled out of my mouth of their own accord. It was a lie more terrible than any I had ever told, a lie far worse than any of his. I half expected a bolt of lightning to shoot in through the window and strike me down; I almost wished it would. But, at the same time, I knew it was the right thing to say, the only way I could ever put an end to this. Danny needed to be adored; he wouldn't want to be with anyone who didn't love him absolutely. The slightest doubt about my feelings would be enough to make him loosen his grip.

'I don't believe you, Omi,' he said. 'I know you love me – I felt it in your kiss.'

'Believe what you want.'

Lying to Danny – and to myself – had freed me. Now that I was acting, my true feelings buried, I could say whatever needed to be said. 'The fact is,' I continued, 'I don't feel the way I did.' I remembered the words Mike had used when I'd asked about The Wonderfulls, and added, cruelly, 'Being with you is too much like hard work.'

Danny flinched. 'Tell me right to my face that you don't love me,' he dared, still defiant.

I took a deep breath. It was harder to say a second time. 'I'm sorry, Danny, but I don't love you.'

He began to shake and I couldn't tell whether it was from fear or anger. He had grown so pale that for a moment I was scared he might pass out. Then his face hardened. 'Go on, then,' he said coldly. 'But remember this: no one will ever love you the way that I love you.'

'It's not enough,' I said. And that, at least, was the truth.

I turned and walked away from his bed, as fast as my legs would carry me, but it felt as if the end of the ward was growing further away with each step. Every patient I passed seemed to have Danny's face, to wear his pained expression. Their eyes bore into me, hating me, accusing me.

When I reached the doors, I glanced back. Danny was still sitting up, his eyes vacant, his lips parted as if he were about to speak.

I hesitated. *Just call out my name*, I thought, *and I'll take it all back.* But I knew it was far too late for that. The best that I could hope for was that one day, when he was well, he would understand my reasons and realise that I wasn't a terrible person. He would see that I did love him after all. Painful as it was, I had to believe that.

He said nothing.

So I pushed open the doors and walked out into the cold, brightly lit corridor to see what life without Danny had in store for me.

Epilogue

I never saw Danny again.

Mike kept in touch with me just long enough to let me know that Danny had gone to the private clinic his mother had told me about, and that he had done well there. The last I heard, he was planning to go back to university and finish his degree.

I hope he is still writing songs and playing, somewhere. It's possible, I suppose, that he has given it all up and joined the rat race he so despised. Maybe he now wears a suit every day and goes to work for his father's company. I'd like to think that isn't true, that at least some part of the person I loved remains.

For a long time, I would watch music shows on TV with some trepidation, in case the next new band to be featured was fronted by Danny. I know it's selfish, but to my relief, it never happened. I often think how awful it must be to have loved someone famous, to have constant reminders of them forced upon you every day.

Perhaps it makes no difference. Once a lover has imprinted himself on your mind, it is impossible to wipe him clean. I can go for weeks, months even, without thinking of Danny and then something – a phrase, or a smell, or a joke – will conjure him up again, as clearly as if I'd seen him the day before. Occasionally, he will feature in my dreams, and I will wake wondering if I did the right thing, feeling guilty for abandoning him, hoping that he has forgiven me. I'm happy now, but if things had turned out differently, could I have been happier?

If I know anything at all, I know this: I will never forget Danny. He has left a D-shaped scar on my heart, just as real as the O-shaped scar he will always wear on his arm.

Acknowledgements

Many thanks to: Brenda Gardner, Yasemin Uçar, Melissa Patey and everybody at Piccadilly; my agent, Janice Swanson at Curtis Brown; Celia Duncan, Diane Leeming and everyone at *CosmoGIRL!*; Bibi Lynch for being my first critic; Nula Bealby for putting up with me; Mum and Dad for the peaceful writing week in France; Matt Whyman for his wisdom and experience; and all my friends for listening and being there. Love and thanks to my husband, Steve Somerset, for the song lyrics for 'Take It Now'. And finally, a bittersweet thanks to all the Dannys I have known, loved and lost.

www.piccadillypress.co.uk

☆ The latest news on forthcoming books

☆ Chapter previews

☆ Author biographies

☆ Fun quizzes

☆ Reader reviews

☆ Competitions and fab prizes

☆ Book features and cool downloads

☆ And much, much more . . .

Log on and check it out!

Piccadilly Press